A DANGEROUS DECEPTION

Cassandra has no option but to flee from her home when pressure is put on her to marry her simple cousin. Masquerading as a governess she removes to Suffolk to teach the lonely daughter of an irascible, yet decidedly attractive, widower. Soon she's in danger of falling in love with Jonathan Anderson — but is she the only one hiding a secret? And will deception keep them apart?

FENELLA MILLER

A DANGEROUS DECEPTION

Complete and Unabridged

LINFORD
Leicester

First published in Great Britain in 2009

First Linford Edition
published 2009

British Library CIP Data

Miller, Fenella-Jane.
  A dangerous deception- -
  (Linford romance library)
  1. Governesses- -England- -Suffolk- -Fiction.
  2. Widowers- -England- -Suffolk- -Fiction.
  3. Deception- -Fiction. 4. Love stories.
  5. Large type books.
  I. Title II. Series
  823.9'2–dc22

ISBN 978–1–84782–795–1

Published by
F. A. Thorpe (Publishing)
Anstey, Leicestershire

Set by Words & Graphics Ltd.
Anstey, Leicestershire
Printed and bound in Great Britain by
T. J. International Ltd., Padstow, Cornwall

This book is printed on acid-free paper

1

Cassandra had always known her name was unlucky and now she was sure of it. This morning her uncle had issued her with an ultimatum: she was to marry her cousin Peregrine or he would not be answerable for the consequences. Cassandra knew what this meant. Her uncle, Sir James Digby, would not dare to incarcerate her in her room on bread and water, not after the last time he'd attempted it and she'd almost starved to death and still wouldn't capitulate. However, she knew that between them her aunt and uncle would make poor Perry's life a misery.

He was a dear boy and she loved him as a cousin, but if he had ever had two consecutive sensible thoughts, she would eat the cherries on her best bonnet. No — not even to save Perry would she be browbeaten into marriage with him.

She had no alternative. She would have to remove herself from Upton Manor. She had already formulated a plan for when this eventuality arose. The pressure on her to agree to become betrothed to Peregrine had been growing these past few months and now it was scarcely nine months to her majority, it was intensifying. Sir John was determined to get hold of her inheritance one way or the other.

Her companion and governess, Ann Roberts, had been summarily dismissed a year ago, but had found a small cottage in the village to rent. It was Cassie's intention to buy a small estate as soon as she was one and twenty and then reside there with Ann, who had become, during the five years they had been together, her best friend and mentor.

She had no intention of getting married. She had been obliged to watch this institution destroy her parents' happiness. They had both caught the fever and died whilst travelling abroad, but her mother had only accompanied her father because she had had no choice. They had been kind and supportive parents but had made each other miserable. It had not been an arranged mariage — they had fallen in love — but still it had been a disaster. She had no intention of involving herself in such a union; as a wealthy heiress she would be courted for her money. Her intelligence and high spirits would be considered a necessary evil. A love match was also out of the question — look what it had done to her parents.

Quickly, she donned her cloak and stout walking boots, then, snatching up her oldest bonnet, a warm muffler and gloves, she headed for the back stairs. She knew the servants were well disposed towards her, and would not report her exit from the side door unless asked a direct question about her whereabouts.

A blast of cold November air whipped her cloak around her as she hurried, head down, through the park and out of the side gate, the quickest way to the village. When she arrived thirty minutes later she was much warmer than when she had left. Her aunt did not allow her to have a fire in her chambers at Upton Manor.

She was almost blown down the short path that led to the front door of Ann's cottage. Cassie knocked loudly. Molly, a young girl from the village and Ann's sole servant, appeared, mob cap, as always, awry. The girl bobbed a curtsy and smiled.

'Come in, Miss Forsythe. Miss Roberts is in the parlour and there's a nice fire burning, I can tell you. Shall you be staying for luncheon, miss?'

Cassie removed her cloak and other things and passed them to Molly. 'I expect so, for I shall get nothing if I go back.'

Ann Roberts, a woman with an unremarkable face but a neat figure and a pair of fine blue eyes, was in her thirtieth year. She had been with Cassie, first as governess and then as companion, until being obliged to leave her position. 'Come in, my dear Cassie, I didn't expect you today as the weather is so inclement. But you're most welcome indeed. I am sad company, I'm afraid, as I'm suffering from a severe head cold.' This last remark was punctuated by a series of sneezes and coughs.

'I had to come, Ann. It has happened, as we expected. I have to get away, and am hoping we can now put the scheme into action.'

'I have been studying the advertisements in The Times this past week, my dear, and I think I have exactly the position for you. Look, one Jonathan Anderson Esquire, requires a governess-companion for his nine year old daughter. They live somewhere outside Ipswich which, I am reliably informed by the vicar, is in a county in the east of the country called Suffolk. I'm sure you would be quite safe there for the next nine months.'

'Excellent. All I have to do is place

the correct name at the start of the letter and sign the bottom. It will be a strange experience for me, being you. I only hope I have learnt enough these past years to bring the deception off successfully.'

'I'm certain no-one will suspect that you're not who your references say you are, my love. The dresses and other things that you will need for your new life are also ready. All I have to do is post the application this afternoon.'

'What if Mr Anderson rejects me? Or demands an interview? It would be impossible for me to get away from Upton to attend one. It will be difficult enough to do it once, but twice? Never.'

Ann patted Cassie's hand. 'Don't fret so, my love. You will not be expected to travel all that way, my papers are impeccable — he would be mad not to snap you up. I'm certain not many well qualified governesses would wish to work so far way from Town.'

'I pray that you're correct. How long will it be, do you think, before we hear?'

'A week, perhaps a little longer. Can you endure for that long, my dear?'

Cassie sighed. 'I have no choice. Perhaps if I appear to be weakening in my resolve it will be bearable.'

'In that case, Cassandra, you must forget all about your problems and look forward to your future.'

They were interrupted by the arrival of a tray containing two steaming mugs of chocolate and a plate of freshly baked scones. Molly was young, but showed signs of being an excellent cook.

'Molly, it seems we might be on the move in ten days. Are you still willing to accompany us?'

'Yes, miss. There's nothing here for me. I'm looking forward to seeing a bit of the world. Do you know where we might be going?'

Ann shook her head. 'It could be in Suffolk, but be sure I'll let you know as soon as we are certain.' The girl curtsied and vanished in a swirl of crisp white apron. 'When we receive a reply

7

from Mr Anderson I'll book the coach for you and Molly. Even if all this comes out one day your reputation will not be tarnished.'

'Why do I care about that? I have no intention of seeking a husband in the *ton*. I am eagerly anticipating the adventure — however poor my accommodation and conditions as a governess, they could not be worse than Upton Manor, and I shall be an independent woman paid for my services, not expected to work for nothing.'

'Exactly. And remember, I shall rent a cottage as close as possible so that you can visit on your afternoon off.' She reached out and showed Cassie an advert she had ringed in blue. 'See, I have already written to this address enquiring about properties in the correct neighbourhood.'

Satisfied that every eventuality had been thought of, the two friends settled back for a comfortable day chatting in front of a warm fire. When Cassie eventually departed it was to run down to mail the letter. She prayed it would remove her from her miserable existence as little more than an unpaid servant at the beck and call of both her aunt and uncle.

* * *

The unrelenting tedium of her daily duties gave Cassie too much time to ponder. She did her best to ignore the constant strident demands from both relations that she should do as she was bid and agree to marry her cousin. Perry was a handsome young man of two and twenty who occupied his time with hunting and shooting — and when the weather was inclement, staring blankly at the fire. He had never been to London, indeed, had no wish to do so. All he wanted from life was to be left alone to live peacefully with his beloved dogs and horses. He was pleasant and dutiful, but sadly lacking in intelligence. Cassie did her best to cheer him up, promising him he should not be forced into marrying her, that everything should be all right in the end. However, she did not dare tell him of her plans knowing he would blurt them out at the first opportunity.

She was in the vestibule preparing to walk down to see Ann on the tenth day after she had posted the letter when Sir John accosted her.

'Well, miss, gallivanting to the village again, I see? Is there nothing you can do to help your aunt?'

Cassie dipped a curtsy and pinned a smile on her thin face. 'No, uncle, I have finished my daily chores and Lady Digby has given me leave to go. Is there anything I can fetch you from the village whilst I'm there, sir?'

'Don't toady to me, young lady, I know your game. You'll do as you're told eventually, unless you want to see your cousin suffer.'

Cassie watched him stomp off, his heavy jowls flushed with anger. Although he had never actually raised his hand to her, she knew if she continued to defy him it might come to that. She didn't know how she would withstand physical attack; she had coped with a cold room, meagre food, and hand-me-down clothes for the past few years, but being beaten? She wasn't sure she was brave enough to continue to defy them if it came to that.

It was unfair. She knew her parents had left her very well-to-do — the interest alone from her trust fund was enough to keep the whole household in luxury and yet she was forced to live like a poor relation.

She tied her muffler snugly round her neck, pulled on her darned gloves and made sure her bonnet was firmly attached to her head before running outside to brave the blustery rain and icy winds.

She'd had a good feeling about this morning, as though her prayers were about to be answered. Indeed, she had almost skipped out of her cold bed so eager was she to get down to Ann's cottage and see if the long-awaited letter had arrived.

Hurrying down the flagstone path twenty minutes later, she saw Ann's face in the window beaming and waving a piece of paper. The reply had come, and it must be a positive response.

Molly had the open before Cassie reached the doorstep. 'Oh, miss, it's come, and they want you. You've to leave immediately, he said as he's booked two tickets on the mail for this very afternoon.'

'Thank you, Molly. I shall go in to Miss Roberts to hear the news.'

The girl blushed, realising she had overstepped the mark. She bobbed a curtsy and dashed off down the corridor leaving Cassie to announce herself.

'Come in, my dear, the letter has come as I am sure Molly has told you. I have managed to book the carter. He will arrive one hour from now to transport you both, and your trunks, to the Fiddler's Arms. You will not be able to go back to Upton Manor, you cannot risk missing the coach. Do you have everything you wish to take with you?'

Cassie smiled as she removed her cloak revealing that she had her reticule and a soft cloth bag slung around her shoulder. 'I have everything I need in here, I brought them today because I just knew the letter would come.'

'Well done. Now, we must go upstairs and get you changed into your new clothes. Molly has gone to get herself ready. Hopefully I shall follow you at the end of the week. You will have to make the journey with only Molly for company. Do you think you shall manage without mishap?'

'Of course I shall. I know I have not been to London since I was a girl, but I'm quite capable of using my tongue. Can I see the letter? Does Mr Anderson seem like a pleasant man?'

Ann handed her the single sheet and a bold black scrawl seemed to leap from the paper. Cassie smoothed it out and read the contents aloud.

Dear Miss Roberts,

I am in receipt of your application and your references are satisfactory. Therefore I should like to offer you the position as governess to my daughter Amanda. I have enclosed the funds necessary for your travelling expenses. I have reserved two seats, as requested, on the mail coach leaving from Barchester at 11 o'clock on the thirteenth of November. Overnight accommodation has been secured for you at the Green Man where you catch the mail coach at nine o'clock on the fourteenth. This takes you directly to Ipswich. I shall make arrangements for you and your maid servant to be collected.

Jonathan Anderson Esq.

'He doesn't seem overjoyed at the thought of making my acquaintance, does he?'

'My dear, he's to be your employer not your bosom bow. Come now, don't look so downcast. He has done all, indeed more, than most employers, to ensure your comfort. He has not caviled at the extra expense of a seat for Molly has he?'

'No, that's quite true. And whatever he's like it's immaterial — he cannot be more unpleasant than Sir John and Lady Digby.'

The rest of the morning sped by and before she knew it she was sitting beside the carter, her trunk in the back, her carpetbag clutched on her lap and Molly beside her. She hoped she would never be obliged to return to Upton Manor, or see her uncle and aunt again.

She was pleased to discover their tickets were for inside seats. Cassie had dreaded the prospect of travelling on the roof for it looked perilous and extremely cold. She had heard stories that passengers had frozen to death up there in the winter months. The yard was bustling with passengers waiting, as they were, for the coach and Molly pressed close to her side, obviously finding the whole experience overwhelming.

'Don't look so scared, Molly, everything will be just as we planned. You should be excited, you're going to see London, albeit only a small part of it, but your horizons are about to widen dramatically. Your life shall never be the same after this morning.'

'That's what I'm afraid of, miss. What if Mr Anderson don't let you keep a maid of your own? Where shall I go until Miss Roberts comes?'

'I'm sure my new employer will allow you to remain with me until Miss Roberts can arrive and take you back into her care. After all he has been generous enough to pay your expenses.'

'I wonder what sort of place we're going to be living in, miss? That letter was written on good quality paper, so maybe he's very well-to-do.'

'Whatever it's like, Molly, I'm sure my life cannot be any worse than it has been these past three years. I shall have my own room, hopefully a fire, and sufficient to eat. I have become so thin, even the extra food you cook me has not made up for the deprivations in my diet. I'm sure I must look like a beanpole.'

The coach rattled into the yard and further conversation was impossible. They were bundled inside, their trunks stowed on the back as the ostlers raced about changing the horses. In less than ten minutes the exchange was done and they were on their way.

Cassie settled back in the corner, Molly close beside her, and glanced round at the other occupants. Opposite her was a soldier in scarlet regimentals. He favoured her with one dismissive glance and resumed his perusal of the countryside. Next to him was a stout farmer's wife and in the remaining space a very thin cleric squashed hard against the window. She turned her head a little to see along the seat on her side. In the remaining seat was a harassed young woman with a baby on her lap and two fractious small children peering out of the window.

She smiled to herself and thought it

17

might be an eventful journey. She felt sure that her skills as a governess would be sorely tried before she reached their destination.

2

The coach trundled into the Green Man long after darkness had fallen. Cassie was the first to emerge and was surprised to find the courtyard almost as bright as day. Flambeaux flickered from the walls and lit up the space with a golden glow. Molly jumped down beside her. Her initial nervousness had faded as the day passed, and she was now as eager as her mistress to enjoy the new sights.

'Shall I stay here and make sure they bring the right trunks in, Miss Roberts?' For a moment Cassie didn't respond, but a sharp nudge on the arm reminded her it was she who was being addressed.

'Yes, Molly, please do that. I shall venture inside and discover which rooms we have been allocated for the night. I am sharp set, I hope they have kept some supper for us.'

* * *

The next morning a steady rain fell from leaden skies and dampened Cassie's enthusiasm for the forthcoming journey into darkest East Anglia. She had passed a comfortable night in a clean, if frugal, chamber, and had eaten a hearty supper of meat pasty and apple pie.

'Shall we break our fast in the parlour downstairs, or have it sent up here as we did last night?'

'Well, I reckon the food will be more plentiful and hotter in the dining room,' Molly answered from the floor, where she was carefully checking the bags were packed and locked and the trunks securely buckled.

After eating, they climbed into the mail coach with only three other passengers, the young officer, and a woman of indeterminate age dressed similarly to her. Cassie had realised early in the journey that being poorly dressed and plain made one almost invisible. She had noticed Molly had received several admiring glances from the ostlers and pot-boys, but she had been overlooked.

For this she was grateful, she had no wish to be ogled by strange gentleman; it suited her new persona to be seen as a nondescript governess. If her travelling companions had known she was a substantial heiress she felt sure she would have been treated with far more courtesy.

She and Ann had discussed her lack of looks on several occasions. She had used to be an attractive girl, with abundant, shining russet brown hair, sparkling hazel eyes and a well rounded figure. But the past years living at Upton Manor had reduced her to the state she was. It suited her for the moment though — no one expected a governess to be attractive.

As the coach rattled through the streets of London she barely listened to Molly's excited chatter from her position in the window seat. Cassandra was dreaming about the day when she could have new clothes, and take her place in society where she belonged.

The journey was long and tedious, the intermittent rain not assisting their passage. They stopped for refreshments at Romford and Colchester, finally arriving at their destination in Ipswich two hours later than the scheduled time. Cassie was worried that Mr Anderson would have recalled his servant long ago and she would be forced to overnight at an inn for the second time.

The mail coach had stopped to change horses and allow the passengers a twenty minute break before completing the journey to Norwich. Cassie stood with Molly by their trunks and carpet bags hoping that someone would step forward from the milling crowd and claim them. They had been standing outside in the drizzle for a quarter of an hour when a tall figure in a many-caped driving coat and a beaver hat pulled low over his ears appeared from inside the inn.

'Here you are! Have you no sense woman? Did it not occur to you to come in and announce yourself? I've been kicking my heels here the best part of two hours, and now you have wasted a further fifteen minutes.'

Cassie was not sure whether to be offended at his brusque treatment or relieved that Mr Anderson had waited for her. Hastily she dipped a curtsy and keeping her eyes demurely down answered softly. 'I do apologise, sir, I assumed that as we were so late, whoever had come to collect us would also be out here. I had no idea you intended to come in person.'

He snapped his fingers and two ostlers leapt forward pulling their forelocks. 'Put the ladies' trunks in my carriage and tell my driver to come round at once.'

Mr Anderson turned to stare down at her. 'You're not what I expected, Miss Roberts, but as long as you are as good as your references, I shall have no complaint.'

He turned his back on her and she felt an urge to poke out her tongue in a childish gesture. It was hardly her fault she was tired and travel worn, or that she was tall and thin. She had not expected to be greeted with open arms, but neither had she expected to be dismissed so summarily.

She felt Molly tugging at her sleeve. 'Miss Roberts, he's a fine looking man, isn't he? A bit of tartar, mind, but I like a man who knows what he's doing, don't you?'

Cassie looked at her maid in astonishment. Molly was barely sixteen years old, when had she acquired such decided preferences about members of the opposite sex? She frowned, hoping to prevent the girl from further indiscretions which might be overheard by her formidable employer.

'Enough of that, if you please, Molly. Remember your place, I have no wish to hear your opinions on such a matter.'

Molly giggled, obviously not impressed at her attempt to be firm. Cassie's lips twitched and she had to bite them to prevent herself joining in. A handsome carriage rolled round from the rear of the inn and a groom jumped down to open the door and pull out the steps. Mr Anderson climbed in leaving Cassie and Molly to follow. She was reminded forcibly that a governess did not warrant the courtesies of a wellborn lady. A gentleman would never have got in in front of *her*, of that she was certain.

The interior of the coach was dark, for which she was grateful. She had no wish to be stared at and found wanting. The journey through the darkness took over an hour, the past twenty minutes of which had been since they'd entered through an imposing pair of wrought iron gates. They were obviously in the carriage of a wealthy man with a large estate. She just hoped his staff were more welcoming than he was.

Ann had explained to her in great detail that a governess was above the servants but not quite one of the family. She would be expected to dine with them, but not attend dinner parties and other social events unless it was to make up the numbers. However she must not fraternise below stairs, although taking a dish of tea with the housekeeper would be acceptable occasionally. This meant that unless Mrs Anderson employed a companion, she would be isolated, neither fish nor fowl.

Cassie straightened her shoulders, feeling to check her bonnet was straight. The wheels crunched over gravel and then the vehicle halted with a jolt. Instantly the groom appeared at the door. She smiled. Unless her employer was prepared to trample over her, this time she would descend first.

It was hard to see the size of house she was to live in for the next year, but if the wide marble steps and pillared portico were anything to go by, this was a substantial and very modern property. She knew that governesses entered by the front door so she waited politely for

Mr Anderson to step past and lead the way. The front door was open and bright candlelight spilled out in a golden arc.

She carried her reticule, leaving Molly to stagger behind with the two carpetbags. The trunks would be transported to whatever space she'd been allocated. Stepping into the house she gazed around in wonderment. The hall was so large you could almost hold a ball in it, she decided. The black-and-white floor gleamed with loving attention and a magnificent pink marble staircase curved up to a gallery in which she could see the wall sconces were lit.

A woman, grey hair scraped back in a severe bun and dressed entirely in black, glided forward. 'Miss Roberts, I am Mrs Green, the housekeeper. You are considerably later than we expected, so I have had a tray left for you. If you'll follow me, I shall conduct you to your rooms.'

Cassie looked round, but the tall dark

man had vanished leaving her to make her own way. Well, that was only to be expected, after all, she was only a governess, not worthy of his attention. She supposed she should be grateful he had come to meet her in person, many employers would not have shown that courtesy.

The housekeeper was already on the staircase and she was obliged to hurry in order to catch up. They went up past the first floor, which was presumably family and guest bedchambers. She knew that the reception rooms were likely to be on the ground floor in such a recent house. They continued up to the second. She was pleased to see that this was also well lit. The decorations were handsome and the floor carpeted in the same style as the lower level.

Mrs Green halted outside a double door. The footman who had been following silently jumped forward and opened the doors with a flourish. Mrs Green stepped in and Cassie followed.

'This is your private sitting room,

Miss Roberts. As you can observe, it's well appointed and you have your own chambermaid to keep it tidy and look after the fires. If you lack anything send her to fetch it.' She marched across the pretty floral carpet and pushed open a door on the far side of the room. 'This is your bedchamber, and there's a box room leading from the dressing room that your abigail can use.'

'Thank you, Mrs Green. It all looks delightful. It is wonderful to find such a warm fire burning and so many candles provided throughout the house.'

For the first time the woman looked directly at her and Cassie saw something flicker in her eyes that could have been sympathy. 'Whatever you have been used to in your previous employment, Miss Roberts, I can assure you that *here* you will be well looked after. Mr Anderson is an excellent employer and would not have it otherwise.' With a hint of a smile the woman swept out, bombazine skirts rustling around her.

Cassie waited until the door clicked shut before turning to Molly her eyes shining with excitement. 'Molly, just look at this. It's better than I've had in the past three years. Such a lovely applewood fire, and look, there's more logs and a bucket of coal beside for later on. I'm going to explore my bedchamber and see where they've put you.'

The bedchamber was equally luxurious, and also had a fire burning merrily in the grate. The large tester bed had pretty floral hangings that matched the curtains at the windows. The room was well appointed also, with occasional tables, a *chaise-longue* by the window and two matching upholstered armchairs.

There was a thumping and banging coming from behind a small door on the left hand side of the room.

'Here, Molly, take my cloak and go and see what all that racket is.'

Molly grinned. 'I reckon it's the trunks coming up, there must be a passageway along the side of that wall. You go and eat your supper, miss, I'll see to everything else. Then I'll nip downstairs and see what the rest of the staff are like. Mrs Green seems fair.'

* * *

The rattle of her curtains being drawn back and the sweet smell of chocolate woke Cassie the next morning. Sleepily, she pushed herself upright and was greeted by the smiling face of a young woman quite unknown to her.

The woman dipped a curtsy and smiled. 'Morning, Miss Roberts, I'm to look after you. I'm Mary, anything you want you just have to ask me.'

'Good morning, Mary. Such luxury, to have two people to take care of me. Where's Molly?'

'Molly's filling your bath, miss, she thought you would like one after your long journey.'

Mary placed a tray across her lap and she looked down with delight. As well as the hot chocolate, there were freshly baked rolls, sweet butter and strawberry preserve. She could not remember the last time she'd had her breakfast brought to her on a tray. She rather thought it wasn't since she was a child and her parents had been alive.

'This looks quite delicious, Mary. I find that I'm quite hungry. Could you tell Cook that her supper last night was most enjoyable?'

'I'll do that, Miss Roberts. Mrs Green said as you needs feeding up, and Cook loves a challenge.'

The girl bustled off about her duties leaving Cassie to rest in her nest of pillows and enjoy her breakfast. A cheerful fire burnt in the grate, as it had done the previous night, and the room was warm and comfortable. She could hardly believe that for the first time in years she would be able to dress without freezing.

She glanced at the mantle clock relieved to see it was only a quarter past seven. She had been sent a message to be in the schoolroom at eight-thirty to meet Miss Amanda.

Dressed in a crisp grey cambric gown, with high neck and long sleeves, she felt ready to start her duties. Molly had arranged her hair in a bun on the nape of her neck, because she knew that it added five years to her appearance, even if it was decidedly unflattering.

'Thank you, Molly. I think I am ready to meet Miss Amanda Anderson.'

Molly shook out the remaining creases in her gown and stood back, her head tilted on one side. 'Mrs Green is right, Miss Roberts, you're far too thin. But I reckon living here will soon make you right.'

Cassie shook her head in despair. However hard she and Ann had tried, Molly found it impossible to curb her tongue, and said exactly what she was thinking, regardless of how inappropriate it might be.

'I would like you to launder the clothes I travelled in, Molly and get them dry and pressed. If you haven't finished unpacking my trunk and pressing the garments from it, you could do that as well. Apart from that I suggest that you get to know the house and the other staff. Perhaps, as it doesn't appear to be raining today, Miss Amanda and I shall be able to go out for a walk later on and I shall require you to accompany us.'

'Yes, miss, that's hardly anything at all. Shall I offer to help out downstairs, if they need me?'

'Yes, of course; if you wish to, ask Mrs Green if there's anything you can do when you've finished my chores.'

Mary was waiting to take her along to the schoolrooms. It seemed that Miss Amanda had her rooms on the same floor as she did, so it was a mere three doors and a short length of passageway to her destination.

Mary vanished through a hidden door in the panelling leaving Cassie standing alone. She stiffened her spine and fixed a friendly smile on her face before pushing open the door. The room was empty. She looked at the mantle clock, it was exactly the time she had been instructed to meet her charge. Well, perhaps the child had overslept; she must allow her a little leeway on their first morning.

She wandered about the room picking up books and looking at the spines, glad to see there were as many storybooks as books of information. There was a board for her to write on, and chalk and duster close by. There were slates, paper and drawing and painting materials.

There was even a handsome globe on a wooden stand by the window. She spun it with one finger, seeing the names of faraway places flash before her eyes, regretting that she would never have the opportunity to see them for herself. The room, like the rest of the huge establishment, was sparkling clean. The desk and her own table were polished to a high shine, and the curtains at the window, although made from a plain navy blue material, looked freshly washed. All the chairs had cushions on their seats which were made of matching stuff.

She had examined every article in the spacious room and still her pupil did not arrive. This was not a good start, she would have to go and find her. She glanced at the clock for the fourth time and saw that it was now a little after nine o'clock. Why had no-one come to explain to her why Miss Amanda was tardy? She might only be a governess, but she should be shown respect, especially from the child she was supposed to be responsible for.

She walked across to the bell strap and pulled it sharply. Five minutes later Mary appeared, an anxious frown on her open features. 'Is something wrong, miss?'

'Miss Amanda has not arrived. She is now thirty-five minutes late. Could you please conduct me to her chamber?'

'But. Miss Roberts, she's downstairs waiting for you with Mr Anderson.

They've been in the library for ever so long.'

Cassie felt sick. She was so sure she'd been told to be in the schoolrooms, but she must have got it wrong. It was she who was late, disastrously so. 'Mary, please conduct me to the library. Mr Anderson will be so angry and I had wanted to make a good impression.' She knew it was inappropriate to discuss such things with the staff, but she had spoken out loud without thinking.

'Come along. Miss Roberts, I'll take you down. It's a misunderstanding, nobody's fault. I'm sure the master will understand.' The girl smiled. 'Miss Amanda's a sweet child, poor motherless mite, she'll not mind how late you are, as long as you're here. She's been that desperate to have a new governess, since the last one left in such a hurry three months ago.'

3

Cassie scarcely noticed the startled expressions of a footman, and Foster the butler, as she ran past, one step behind Mary. The house was so spacious it took them a further five minutes to reach their destination. The library door was open and she could hear the soft murmur of voices inside. She paused, trying to steady her ragged breathing and Mary quickly shook out her skirts and gave her a sympathetic smile.

With a shaking hand Cassie tapped nervously on the door. She expected an answer barked from Mr Anderson, but instead she heard the light treble of a child's voice.

'Papa, here she is. Someone must have gone to fetch her.' Running footsteps came towards her and the door swung back to reveal a girl with blonde ringlets and pale blue eyes. The child dipped in a careful curtsy.

'Miss Roberts, please do come in, we were becoming anxious and thought perhaps you were unwell this morning. I have been so looking forward to meeting you, did you have a good journey?'

The carefully rehearsed greeting was repeated with a happy smile. It was hard to be nervous when greeted with such affection. Cassie took the proffered hand in hers and smiled down at her charge.

'Thank you for making me so welcome, Miss Amanda. I can assure you that I am delighted to be here. I must apologise for my tardiness.' She paused and looked up at Mr Anderson who was standing with his back to the fire, his face stern and uncompromising. 'I had been under the misapprehension that I was to wait in the schoolroom, I have been doing so since thirty minutes past eight. It is only now that I've discovered my error. It's not a good start and

I beg your pardon most sincerely.'

Did she detect a slight thaw in his expression? 'Schoolroom? Amanda, can you remember what you wrote in your note to Miss Roberts?'

Cassie felt the hand in hers twitch. 'I'm sorry, Papa, but I cannot remember. I thought I had said the library, but it is very likely that I said the schoolroom, I was so excited when I wrote it that I could have put the stable and then where would we be?'

'I see — well there's no harm done, but I believe that you owe Miss Roberts an apology?'

Amanda grinned up at Cassie. 'I apologise, Miss Roberts, and I'll explain how it happened later.'

Puzzled by this cryptic answer Cassie nodded. 'I think it's best if we forget all about it, Miss Amanda.'

She had in her hand an outline of the subjects she intended to teach her charge, the hours in which these studies would take place, and how the other times in the day would be occupied.

She offered them to Mr Anderson, but he shook his head.

'No, Miss Roberts, I shall leave my daughter's education in your capable hands. I am away on business a great deal, and need to have a responsible adult here in my absence. The housekeeper and butler take care of the staff and I have an excellent estate manager, but what I don't have is anyone to take care of my daughter. That is to be your role, and as long as Amanda is happy and not running wild about the place then I shall be content.'

Cassie was speechless. She stared, round-eyed, at her employer as though he had just stepped straight from Bedlam. Not interested in his daughter's education? Only concerned with her happiness? That hardly fitted with his stern face and formidable appearance. 'Thank you for your confidence in me, sir, I can assure you I shall not let you down. But what time do you wish to see Miss Amanda each day?'

'I shall see her whenever I can. I shall

come up to the schoolroom when I have time, or Amanda can come and see me if I'm not occupied. We sometimes ride out together in the mornings when I'm here. Do you ride, Miss Roberts?'

It was a long time since Cassie had done so, but as a girl she had been a noted horsewoman. 'I do, but unfortunately I've not had the opportunity recently. I should like to accompany you sometimes, sir, if that's possible.'

'Not only possible, it's essential. Also, when I'm away, I wish you to continue with Amanda's riding.'

Cassie could feel the small hand in hers was shaking and glanced down; where had all the joy gone from the little girl's face? What had her father said to make her quiver with fear? There was more going on here then she understood, but no doubt she would understand after she'd been in his employment for a while.

She drew the child closer to her, slipping her arm around the girl's shoulders. Cassie felt the press of the small body against her hip and knew she had made the right move. 'Do you wish me to dine with you in the evenings, sir? I would prefer to eat with Miss Amanda in the schoolroom.'

'I rarely dine at home, Miss Roberts. However, when I do, I shall require your company. Otherwise you may please yourself.'

She noticed a slight pinching at his nostrils and he appeared to be having difficulty swallowing. There was something very amiss here, but now was not the time to delve into it. Her employer's health problems were not hers, her sole responsibility was for little girl leaning trustingly against her side. She half curtsied and raising her head spoke firmly. 'If that's all, sir, pray excuse us, we are already late starting today's lessons.' She turned swiftly and escorted Amanda from the library feeling his eyes boring in to her back, not knowing what she'd said or done that had caused him so much disquiet.

The morning passed swiftly. She soon discovered that Amanda was an able pupil and eager to learn. Although her father had been disinterested in the timetable, Cassie felt it was important that her pupil knew what to expect each day and what lessons had to be prepared each evening.

Amanda had told her she had a nursemaid and a nanny still in attendance, and that they looked after her in the evening.

'Do you never see your father after supper, Miss Amanda?'

'He's rarely here, Miss Roberts. That's why I told him you were to come to the library when I'd told you to wait in the schoolroom. That way I was certain to have at least some time with Papa. I'm sorry if I made you uncomfortable.'

'I understand absolutely, my dear. You must find every opportunity you can to spend time with Mr Anderson. He is obviously a devoted parent and enjoys your company.' Cassie smiled as she continued. 'Now, about the evenings, you were going to tell me what normally happens here.'

'I always eat my tea in the nursery, and then play with my doll's house or perhaps read. It would be wonderful to eat with you sometimes if that's possible.'

'Is there a small dining room, one that is used just for the family?'

The girl nodded vigorously, her fair ringlets bobbing on her shoulders. 'There is, it's where Papa eats when he's at home. Are you suggesting that we use it when he's not?'

'I am, yes. I hardly think it's fair to ask the staff to carry up trays of food every night if we can bring ourselves downstairs. We can change for dinner and pretend we are grown-ups. I have two smart gowns, do you have something suitable?'

'I do, I have hundreds of gowns; the seamstress in the village is for ever coming to make me fresh ones. Do you know there are some hanging in my closet that I've never worn and never will, as I've already grown out of them.'

They went downstairs to luncheon which was served in the breakfast parlour. It consisted of cold cuts, warm pasties, fruit and buttermilk, more than adequate for a midday repast, Cassie thought. After lunch was a time for recreation. She had planned to go for a walk but the weather outside made that impossible.

'Shall we go back up to the nursery, Miss Amanda, and you can show me what games you have, or perhaps you would like to play a game of hide and go seek?' This last suggestion was greeted with squeals of delight.

So the day passed and the more time she spent with her charge the more Cassie loved her. There had been no mention of the mother, when she'd died or how, and she did not feel she knew Amanda well enough to question her. One thing she had discovered was that the child was quite happy to stay indoors, in fact positively revelled in the bad weather. The last thing she said as they embraced before retiring that evening was that she hoped it was still raining in the morning.

Cassie returned to her apartment with a lot of things to consider. She had been so busy all day there had hardly been time to think about what pandemonium might be taking place back at Upton Manor. Her disappearance would have been noted two days since, but would her uncle have sent out the constables to search for her? He would be in a black rage, of that she was certain.

He hated to have his plans thwarted, and would know that once his quarry had flown he was unlikely to get his hands on her again. She thought of her cousin Peregrine; he might be having a poor time of it at the moment, but in the future his life would be better. His parents knew his limitations, and that no one else was likely to marry him. Without their captive bride she hoped they would leave him alone to live his simple life.

Should she be worrying about her past? No, she had put that behind her, started a new life here, had a new name and employment in a grand house. In fact, she felt sure that Sir John would give up his search after a few days when he failed to find her and spend the next nine months trying to steal as much as he could from her trust fund whilst he was still her legal guardian.

She and Ann had planned her escape carefully and considered every detail. As soon as she'd taken her friend's name she had become invisible to anyone who didn't know her. If enquiries were ever made in this remote part of the country, Miss Ann Roberts would be the governess not Miss Cassandra Forsyth.

Ann's intention had been to leave the village, ostensibly to take up this employment, but she would arrive in Martlesham as Mrs Davina Harper, the widow of a hero of Waterloo. It had been planned in every particular, no one would be looking for a Mrs Davina

Harper, they would be looking for a Miss Cassandra Forsythe. Their plan, in her opinion, was faultless.

All she had to do was remain in her post the full nine months until her majority, when Sir John would no longer be her guardian and she would be safe from coercion, a free and independent woman. She would finally gain control of her fortune and be able to set up her own establishment. It did not occur to her that uncle might be more astute than she had given him credit for and would suspect that her sudden disappearance was connected in some way to Ann's movements . . .

Mr Anderson left on business in London two days after Cassie's arrival at the Hall and she felt a definite relaxing in the atmosphere, as if everyone had been on their best behaviour whilst he was present. The staff smiled more readily, and even the austere butler was seen to have a lightening of expression.

Cassie had been in residence a week

and was desperate to get down to the village which was a little over a mile away. Ann must have arrived and be settled in her new home by now. Although she wasn't sure which property Ann had chosen to rent, it shouldn't be difficult to enquire in the village for a friend called Mrs Harper.

There had been three to select from so all Cassie had to do was send Molly to visit each of the addresses and see if her friend had arrived. The plan had been that Ann would leave as soon as she could arrange a seat on the coach. Surely that would have been only a day or two after her own departure?

There had been no more mention of riding and, remembering how Amanda's hand had shaken in hers at the mention of horses, Cassie decided not to insist that they go on horseback. Instead she suggested that they reverse the order of their day; do their lessons in the afternoon and take their constitutional that morning.

'I should like to explore the village,

and this is the first morning the sun has been out. I thought it would be pleasant to walk down that way. I hope you can direct me, for I have no idea the whereabouts of anything as yet.'

Amanda was thrilled at the prospect of walking to the village. 'I do know, Miss Roberts. Nanny sometimes takes me down there. Shall we have time to visit the shops? There is a haberdashers and a general stores and sometimes Papa gives me a coin to spend.'

'Then that is what we shall do. I have sufficient funds to buy you something small. Now, run along and find your thickest cloak and warmest boots — it might be sunny, but I'm sure it's quite chilly outside.'

She heard her pupil running eagerly back to her room and smiled. Amanda was such an easy child to teach, so beautiful, so open natured, she was at a loss to know how such a dark and brooding man had produced this lovely sunny girl.

Molly was ready and waiting when

she got back to her own chambers. 'There you are, miss. I'm that desperate to get out of this house, I can't remember when it's been so long since I had a walk in the fresh air. Here, I've got your boots and things all ready for you.'

It was a matter of moments to don her sturdy boots and lace them firmly, find her muffler and gloves and tie on her serviceable bonnet. She surveyed her appearance in the mirror. 'Do you know, Molly, I believe my colour is already better, and my cheeks filling out a little. I might not have had any fresh air, but living in comfort and eating good food is already having a beneficial effect on me.'

She was just leaving her chamber when Amanda burst into her room. 'Oh good, Miss Roberts, you're ready to leave. Nanny says she would come if you wished her to, but I know she'd rather stay indoors in the warm.'

'Miss Amanda, what did you forget to do?' Cassie remonstrated gently.

The child's face fell. 'I am sorry, Miss Roberts, I should have knocked and waited for you to bid me enter. I beg your pardon.'

'Your apology is accepted, my love. Now, there is no need for Nanny to come with us, Molly is to accompany us. You can call in and tell her as we go past.'

A footman swung open the heavy front door and she emerged blinking, feeling rather like a mole that had been underground too long, into the watery sunlight. She realised she had not been outside since her arrival over a week ago. Taking Amanda's hand in hers she ran lightly down the steps and out on to the gravel turning circle. She stopped and slowly looked around her.

'My word, Miss Amanda, I had no idea how substantial your home is. Do you know, this is the first time I've seen it properly since I arrived last week? I can't imagine how many rooms there must be here. I know you told me your grandfather built this house after the

53

original hall burnt down in a fire, but I didn't think to ask how big it was. Now that I can see for myself, I must own that I am very impressed indeed.'

Amanda jumped up and down in excitement. 'Papa says it is the finest house in the neighbourhood, he's very proud of it.' Her face fell. 'If he loves it so much, why does he spend so much time away from here? Away from me?'

That was a question Cassie would like the answer to herself. Molly had done her best to glean information from the staff, but they had been very close-lipped. All she knew was that Mrs Anderson had died some time ago in an accident, and that there had been three governesses employed since then and none of them had stayed above a few months.

This last fact intrigued her most. What was it about this place that drove these women away? She knew she had luxurious apartments, she was waited on hand and foot as though a real member of the family, and the little girl she was looking after could not be sweeter. So what was it that had caused the previous governesses to depart?

She shivered, as unbidden an explanation insinuated itself into her happiness. There was only one reason she could think of that could explain their premature departure. It had to be something to do with her employer — what did he do that was so awful these women no longer wished to remain under his roof? Was his surly temper and brusque manner the reason?

She frowned as another thought occurred to her. She hadn't liked to enquire, but perhaps the girls had been dismissed, not left of their own volition? Either way, there was a mystery here and she was determined to solve it.

4

The walk to the village took little over half an hour and during that time the weather turned decidedly cold.

'I fear we could be in for some snow, Miss Amanda, so we had better not delay too long. Even though it is not above a mile or so back to the Hall, our route is across an open field and it would be decidedly unpleasant to be caught there in a snowstorm.'

'Mrs Green told Nanny that Fred, the head gardener, thinks there will be snow before the end of the day, but when I got up and saw it was sunny, I thought they had been mistaken so didn't mention it to you.'

The child looked anxious, obviously believing she was at fault. 'There's no need to worry, Miss Amanda, the walk is my decision. If we get caught out in bad weather there will be no one to blame but me.' They were now entering the busy High Street. She noticed that the road was a trifle potholed, but there were flagged paths on either side for pedestrians to use. Cassie was also delighted to see several shops and many other businesses. If the village was prospering then she was sure that Ann would settle in well and that they would both make friends amongst the local populace. She turned to Molly.

'Molly, I wish you to go to those three addresses you have on the paper I gave you this morning. If you find one occupied, knock on the door and make yourself known.'

Molly nodded. 'I'll do that, Miss Roberts, I'll ask at the blacksmith's where each property is situated. Where shall I meet you?'

Cassie looked around. 'I wish to go into the haberdashers, and then the general store. There is an inn, The Black Sheep, further down that looks clean and wholesome. Miss Amanda and I shall wait for you there, I'm sure we can order refreshments of some sort whilst we wait.'

She was surprised that Amanda wasn't greeted by any of the locals, although several people turned to look at them and half smiled, no one actually stopped and spoke. 'Miss Amanda, do you not know anyone in the village? Don't you attend church here on Sundays?'

'No, Miss Roberts, Papa does not approve of the church. I have not been since . . . since my mother died. We rarely went to the village before then, Mama thought it was full of common people and not suitable for me to be here.'

Cassie wanted to ask more, but refrained as they were about to enter a shop. An hour later, purchases complete, she was sitting in front of roaring fire in a neat private parlour at The Black Sheep.

'It looks like it's turning right nasty out there, miss. Is someone collecting you from here?' The jovial landlord

58

spoke to them as he placed the steaming mugs of chocolate down.

'No, we have walked down from Martlesham Hall, I'm just waiting for my maid to come back from an errand, and then we shall walk back.'

The man scratched his bald pate and his smile slipped a little. 'I don't reckon you should risk it, miss, it's a good long walk to the Hall and across open fields. The sea brings an icy wind to this area and when it snows it can soon turn into a blizzard.'

She had been thinking that herself as she watched the heavy grey clouds roll across the sky obliterating the sun. 'I'm afraid we have no choice, landlord, unless you have a vehicle which I can hire to transport us home?'

He shook his head. 'I'm sorry, miss, but I've only the one gig and that's in use at the moment.'

That moment the door opened and Molly came in, her cheeks flushed from the cold. 'Miss Roberts, it's turning really bad out there. If we're going to get home today, I think we'd better leave straight away.'

Hastily Cassie paid for the unfinished drinks and buttoned her charge back into her thick winter coat, tying her bonnet strings securely. Molly then did the same for her.

Five minutes later they were back in the High Street and gusts of icy wind buffeted them back along the pavement. Amanda ran ahead, laughing as the wind whipped her coat open and closed as if unseen hands were snatching at it. Cassie took the opportunity to turn to Molly.

'Did you find her, Molly?'

'No, miss, it's mighty strange — all three properties are occupied, but none of them by you-know-who. I spoke to a Mrs Smith, who moved in yesterday to the cottage on the edge of the green. She told me that she had only been lucky enough to get that cottage because a young widow had cancelled her reservation at the last minute.'

Cassie felt an icy shiver run up her

spine and it wasn't caused by the weather. She had no time to comment as Amanda ran back to her, her face glowing with excitement.

'Isn't this exciting, Miss Roberts? You know, I've never been out in a storm before. Do you think it will snow before we get home? Shall we be like intrepid explorers?'

'I fear that we shall, Miss Amanda. I for one am not overly partial to blizzards, but I'm prepared to enjoy the experience for your sake.'

The child stared at her a moment and then laughed. 'You're funning me, Miss Roberts. I do so like it when you tease.'

Cassie and Molly exchanged glances, the more she got to know her charge, the more there was to discover. The threatened snow started to fall in blustery clouds when they were halfway across the field. Fortunately they reached the shelter of Home Woods before it became too heavy. They paused underneath the overhanging branches to shake out their cloaks and stamp snow from their boots.

'Well, that's the worst of the journey over. Come along, Miss Amanda, let's hold hands and see if we can run the rest of the way. That should warm us up sufficiently so we won't die from the cold.'

The child obediently held out her hand and, gathering up her skirts, Cassie started to increase her pace. They erupted onto the gravel circle at full speed, barely able to see a few yards in front of them through what had now become a blizzard. Breathless they raced round to the side door, which was always left open, and Molly held it back. As it slammed behind them they collapsed in a heap against the wall, laughing and brushing snow from their faces.

Cassie was just about to undo the buttons on Amanda's coat when she heard heavy footsteps approaching rapidly from the front hall.

'Where the devil have you been?

Have you lost your senses, woman? What possessed you to take my daughter out in a blizzard?'

Cassie's hands stilled, but her heart thumped wildly. She glanced up at Amanda's face and saw the fear in it. Some instinct made her grin and a wink immodestly. Slowly she stood up and as she did so she whispered in Amanda's ear. 'Now I'm for it, what bad luck, Mr Anderson arriving just as we were having so much fun together.'

She felt the rigid shoulders under her hands relax. Quickly she pushed the little girl towards Molly and her maid, taking the hint, took the child away, leaving Cassie to turn and face the glowering man.

'We were in no danger, Mr Anderson, the snow did not start until we were in the shelter of the woods. Your daughter does not have nearly enough exercise and a walk to the village, whatever the weather, is good for her.' She risked raising her eyes as she finished her sentence. She wished she hadn't.

'I wish to speak to you in my study. Be there in five minutes.' He raked her with an icy stare then vanished leaving her flustered and unsure of herself. She ran up the back stairs and into her rooms where Molly was waiting.

'I have to change, I have to be in the study in five minutes. I'm in for a bear garden jaw, that's for sure. I cannot understand why Mr Anderson is so enraged. We would hardly have come to any harm even if we had been stuck in the snow. A few strongmen could soon have rescued us before anything untoward occurred.'

'The hem of your gown is mired, miss. If you take off your boots and things, I'll fetch you a clean one. If we're quick, I reckon you can be changed and still back downstairs in a minute or two.'

★ ★ ★

Cassie hesitated outside the study door before knocking. She suspected that

64

Amanda's fear had been for her, not for herself. Did the girl think she would be dismissed for taking her down to the village? She heard the barked command to enter and pushed open the door, determined not to show any nervousness. She had done nothing wrong, her charge had been in no danger, and her employer had given her full responsibility for his daughter's upbringing.

He was standing, one elbow on the mantelshelf, his ankles crossed, his face no longer angry but not friendly either. Cassie curtsied politely and waited, marooned in the middle of the carpet, to be given leave to sit. Slowly he pushed himself upright and gestured at an upright mahogany chair on one side of the fire. Gratefully she settled herself and waited for the tirade to begin. She heard him sigh as he settled himself on the padded sofa.

'I must apologise for raising my voice, I was anxious about Amanda, and fear that I overreacted.'

'You have no need to apologise to

me, sir, I am your employee, you may speak to me as you please.'

She saw a flicker of humour cross his face. 'Good God! Are you telling me you're not offended by my behaviour? You're not going to run away?'

Cassie smiled at him. 'No sir, I am not. I'm merely telling you that you don't have to apologise.'

This time he laughed and the harsh lines of his face softened making him look younger, more approachable, almost handsome. 'Well, I'm glad we've got that settled. I may be as uncivil as I wish, and you shall be suitably offended — that seems remarkably straightforward. I wish all my other dealings were so simple.'

Cassie felt herself warming towards him. He was a man of contradictions, but he obviously loved his daughter, perhaps too much — so why did he abandon her so readily and leave her in the charge of a virtual stranger?

He stretched out his long booted legs stared down at them, lost in private thoughts. This gave Cassie the opportunity to examine him more closely. His features were not regular enough to be called handsome, but when he smiled he was definitely attractive. She thought he was about three and thirty, perhaps a little more; it was hard to tell as the hard plains of his face had no surplus flesh to soften them and this made him, perhaps, appear older than he was.

His breadth of shoulder was impressive, and he must stand two yards high in his stocking feet. A slight smile twitched the corners of her mouth. It was not often she came across a man who could look down on her. As if aware of her scrutiny his head suddenly shot up and she felt herself flush from the soles of the feet to the crown of the head. Instead of being offended he leant forward, as if looking at her more closely.

'Do you like what you see, Miss Roberts? Do I come up to snuff?'

Cassie hung her head in embarrassment. 'I should not . . . I should not have been staring at you in that way, sir, but you must remember we only met once, and that was so brief, I hardly had time to take in your appearance.'

As soon as the words left her mouth she knew they were inappropriate. What possible reason could there be for a lowly governess to be interested in her employer's appearance?

He chuckled, the rich dark sound sending a different kind of shiver up her spine. 'Look at me,' he commanded softly.

She raised her head and found he was disconcertingly close, his direct blue gaze pinning her to her seat in a way that was both uncomfortable yet oddly pleasurable.

'You are far too thin, Miss Roberts. I thought at first that you were plain, but now I see I am mistaken. Did they starve you in your last employment?'

Cassie almost choked. How dare he comment on her appearance in such a familiar way? Then the absurdity of her reaction became apparent. She had only herself to blame — after all, she had been looking at him in exactly the same way.

She settled back in her chair, prepared to enjoy the banter. 'Not quite, sir, but I was always hungry, and rarely warm in the winter. I'm sure with Mrs Green's, and your cook's intervention, I shall soon regain my normal weight.'

He nodded, obviously satisfied with her answer. 'Are you happy here. Miss Roberts? Do you intend to stay more than a few weeks?'

Puzzled, she tilted her head and looked at him in surprise. 'Of course I'm happy here, sir. It is many years since I have been so happy. Your daughter is a delight to teach, my accommodation is as good as anything I could have expected, and my duties are certainly not arduous.'

'And you shall not run screaming from the door if I shout at you occasionally?'

'Shout at me? Good heavens! No, sir,

that is your prerogative. I believe we've got that matter settled — you shall be as rude to me as you wish, and I shall be mortally offended.'

'Excellent! I see we are going to deal well together, Miss Roberts. Now, tell me why you ventured into the village in a snowstorm?' His query was mild, but she saw his eyes were watchful.

'When I left, sir, there was no snow in sight, there was a clear blue sky and bright sunshine. Admittedly it was a trifle cold, but we were well wrapped up and the walk is no more than a mile or so. Your daughter was so excited to be going down there — she was able to buy a candy cane and a new ribbon for her bonnet.'

'I see.' He smiled. Cassie melted into her seat, warmed by the blaze. 'In that case, I understand. Don't worry, I shall not beg pardon, I have learnt how things must be between us.'

She stood, bringing the interview to an end. 'Will you excuse me, sir? I must go back to my charge. She'll be wondering whether ... she will be waiting for me.'

He rose, towering above her, but she no longer found him threatening, merely large. 'As the weather is so bad, I shall be dining at home tonight. I shall expect you to join me. I don't keep country hours here, I prefer to eat late. I shall expect you in the drawing room at six and thirty.'

She curtsied. 'I shall be there.'

Closing the door quietly behind her, she leant on it, allowing her hectic colour to subside. She was not sure if she was looking forward to dining alone with her employer. He seemed far more threatening to her equanimity when he was being charming than when he was roaring and blustering.

5

Later that day the snow became a full scale blizzard and by late afternoon there were several feet of snow in the places where the wind had blown it in from the open fields. Amanda pressed her nose against the steamed up schoolroom window. Cassie heard her sigh deeply.

'I don't suppose we shall be able to go down to the village again for a long while, shall we, Miss Roberts?'

'No, my dear, but at least your Papa will be obliged to remain here and not go away on business.'

The child turned, eyes sparkling with joy. 'I had not thought of that, Miss Roberts. Can I go down and see him now?'

'Well, I see no reason why not, he did say if he was here you could go and find him at any time. I am to dine with him tonight and must repair to my rooms to get ready. I shan't see you again until the morning. When you return from speaking to your father you must go at once to join Nanny, is that clear, Miss Amanda?'

'Of course, I had forgotten you are to dine with Papa. Do you have something more elegant than the dress you have been wearing these past few nights?'

'No, I'm afraid that I don't. I am a governess, Miss Amanda, I do not own an elegant evening gown, it would never be used, even if I could afford to purchase one.'

The child pouted. 'That's a shame, I am sure that Papa would like to see you in something colourful.' Immediately Amanda blushed, believing she had been impertinent. 'I beg your pardon, Miss Roberts. Your grey dresses are very smart, please don't think I am criticising your appearance in any way, but I believe that you would look lovely in moss green, or perhaps an autumn gold?'

Cassie laughed at her pupil's imaginings. She'd never owned such finery; the last time she'd worn a dress that was not plain and serviceable and made from cotton fabric was when she'd been living with her parents, which was almost six years ago. 'I have no such gowns, I'm sorry to say. Perhaps one day I shall own something that grand. My dear, if you're going to go downstairs, you must run along right away. Nursery tea is served in less than an hour, remember, you must not be late.'

She heard Amanda's footsteps clattering back down the passageway. Quickly she tidied the schoolroom. She had asked Molly to have a bath prepared, she was going to wash her hair and dry it in front of the fire then have it dressed in a more becoming style. Although she had no evening gowns of the sort that Amanda spoke of, she did have a lavender muslin, that fell prettily from a high waist and had a sash of purple which set it off nicely.

74

At six thirty precisely she arrived in the entrance hall and waited to be escorted to the drawing room. The butler grandly threw open the door and announced her name as if she was a person of consequence. She saw Mr Anderson look up — he appeared to be as startled as she was by his butler's performance. However, he smiled and his manner was charming, as if he was indeed welcoming a lady into his presence. He stepped forward bowed formally. 'Good evening, Miss Roberts, permit me to say that you look quite charming tonight.'

She dipped in a low curtsy and straightened, her eyes sparkling with excitement. 'You may indeed, sir, it is not often that someone as unimportant as I receives a compliment from such a splendid gentleman.'

'Come now, you're doing it too brown, Miss Roberts. You might be a governess, but I would stake my life on the fact that once you were something else entirely.'

Her breath stopped in her throat. Had she given herself away so easily? She felt a telltale colour rising and quickly turned away as if deciding where to sit. Had he detected her unease? Seen guilt written on her face? She didn't dare to look up, in case he asked a direct question and she was forced to lie.

'Would you like some sherry wine? I think it is vile stuff myself, but ladies seem to like it.'

She settled herself gracefully on an upright wooden chair before answering. 'No thank you, sir, I am of the same opinion. I require nothing at the moment, thank you.'

He sat down opposite, stretching out his legs, his black trousers and evening slippers making his limbs seem even longer.

'Well, that's exhausted that topic of conversation. Now, let me see, what shall I try next? The weather is decidedly unpleasant, don't you think, Miss Roberts?' He stared at her earnestly, a wicked twinkle in his eyes.

She responded in similar style, enjoying the badinage. 'Indeed it is, Mr Anderson. I have never seen snow like it in my life.' Hastily she withdrew a handkerchief from her reticule pretending that she needed to blow her nose. She made a poor job of hiding her giggles. 'Is something wrong, Miss Roberts? Are you unwell in some way? You appear to be having difficulty breathing?' His enquiry was mild, but it was enough to release the pent-up laughter. Cassie was tempted to stuff the handkerchief in her mouth for that was the only way she could think of to prevent her mirth from bursting out. Instead she allowed a gurgle to escape, and looking up at him, shrugged her shoulders. 'I'm sorry, sir . . . ' she spluttered, 'but this is absurd. Why are we pretending to be something we are not?' As soon as she'd spoken, she knew her words were unwise, giving him permission to enquire further into her past.

She was saved from interrogation by Foster appearing at the double doors that led into the dining room. 'Dinner is served.'

Her employer rose and offered her his arm. She was obliged to take it. As she rested her fingers lightly on his forearm she felt his muscles tense at her touch, and something, she didn't understand what, ran through her body making her feel strangely hot and flustered. He escorted her into the dining room and up to a chair to the left of his, which was placed at the head of the enormous table

'There you are, Miss Roberts. I insisted that we sat together as I have no intention of shouting down the table throughout the meal. I hope you approve of the arrangements?'

'It is not my place to say, sir, but I'm sure whatever you arrange everything will be exactly as it should be.' She kept her eyes lowered, not daring to see his expression. A footman jumped forward and assisted her in to her seat, then took out a crisp damask napkin and laid it across her lap. The butler stepped forward and half-filled her crystal glass with deep red wine then, moving with exaggerated dignity, he filled his master's glass to the brim.

'I have dispensed with formality. Miss Roberts.' Cassie's head shot up and looked at him in astonishment. His lips twitched. 'Well, what I should say is that I'm not having several courses with removes. I have selected a simple meal which we shall have served to us. I hope this meets with your approval.'

He stared at, daring her to answer in a similar vein to her previous comment. She grinned. 'As long as there is plenty of it, sir, I have no objection in what order, or what fashion it arrives in front of me.'

His shout of laughter echoed down the large empty room, startling the footman, who slopped soup over the edge of Cassie's bowl on to the pristine tablecloth. The outrage of the butler at such clumsiness made her want to laugh again. She didn't make the mistake of catching the eye of her dining companion. When their bowls were full, the footman and Foster retreated to the far end of the room, almost out of earshot.

She picked up her spoon and before dipping it in aromatic broth sniffed appreciatively. 'It smells quite delicious. You have an excellent cook here, Mr Anderson. I have never eaten so well in my life.'

'And you are already looking better for it, Miss Roberts.'

This time she did meet his glance and what she saw there made her cheeks colour for the second time that night. She dropped her gaze and drank her soup in silence. It was impossible to converse normally, the lurking presence of the butler and footman made her feel uncomfortable.

They didn't eat entirely in silence, however; Mr Anderson made suitable remarks, and she answered politely. But she was relieved when the final dish was finished and she could excuse herself.

'I shall leave you to your port, sir, and thank you for inviting me to dine with you. It has been a most enjoyable experience.'

He stared thoughtfully over the rim of his class. She noticed it had been refilled many times during the meal. 'The evening is not over yet, Miss Roberts. I shall join you very shortly in the drawing room. I shall expect you to be there.'

The ever-present footman pulled back her chair and she sailed from the room, hoping her nervousness was not apparent. She was tempted to make good her escape whilst she still could, but didn't want to risk her employer's wrath. Nervously she paced up and down the carpet when in the corner she spied a pianoforte. Why hadn't she seen the instrument before? She supposed it was because she had only been into the room once, when Amanda had taken her on a grand tour of the house.

She hurried over to the instrument and raised the lid, running her hands lovingly along the polished surface. She glanced over her shoulder, the dining room door was still closed. Perhaps she had time to play something before Mr Anderson joined her.

Music had been her one escape from the drudgery of living with her uncle and aunt at Upton. There was a music room, no warmer than anywhere else she was allowed to go, but when she was free, she retreated there and lost herself in melody. She sat down and closed her eyes, deciding what to play. She didn't need to find any sheets, she had a repertoire of many pieces she could play from memory. As soon as her fingers touched the keys she forgot where she was, who she was, and let the beauty of the sonata carry her away.

She was unaware that he had come into the room, drawing his chair up close to sit behind her, resting his head back and closing his eyes, to enjoy the rare treat of hearing such a wonderful performance. Cassie's hands were finally still, she sat relaxed and smiling on the piano stool blissfully unaware he was watching her so intently, a mere yard or two behind her. She was jerked from her reverie by his mild enquiry.

'I do not remember seeing on your résumé, Miss Roberts, that you are such an accomplished pianist. Why is that, I wonder?'

Cassie carefully closed the lid of the instrument, giving herself time to think of an appropriate answer. The reason it hadn't been on the résumé was because Ann didn't have a musical bone in her body. As she was supposed to be her friend, music should not be part of her repertoire.

She didn't know what to say, she hated telling untruths, had disliked the necessity of becoming an impostor, but the only way she could remain safe until she reached her majority was by impersonating her friend. She came to a decision. There was something about this man that made her believe she could trust him, and in spite of her deception, he might just possibly see why she'd been forced to do it and allow her to stay.

Cassie stood up and walked round him, returning to the upright chair she'd sat on before they dined. She waited until he joined her, placing his own chair disconcertingly close. She took a few steadying breaths then raised her head.

'I have something to tell you, sir, something that I'm ashamed of, and I know that you will be most displeased. I just pray you can understand my motives.' She watched him lean back in his chair folding his arms across his chest; he didn't speak, but he did not look angry, merely interested.

'I am not Ann Roberts. I am Miss Cassandra Forsythe. I am masquerading as my own governess, and it is her résumé that you received. She is unable to play the pianoforte — I had quite forgotten when I sat down in front of it that by playing I would reveal myself.'

'Go on, tell me the rest of your story.'

'My parents died six years ago and I was placed in the care of my maternal aunt, Lady Digby, and her husband. Sir John. They had no wish to look after me, but were pleased to be able to access the interest from my trust fund. I have been kept as little more than an unpaid servant these past few years, whilst they enjoyed my money. They have a son, who is little more than a simpleton, but is gentle and kind. As my majority approaches — I shall be one and twenty next July — they have become more insistent that I marry him.

'The more I refused the more unkind they were to him, making his life unbearable. I am quite able to withstand meagre food and cold chambers, but poor Perry is not made of such strong stuff. He did not understand why they were being unkind to him.' She saw sympathy reflected in his eyes and felt emboldened to continue. 'So

85

you see, sir, I had no choice, I had to remove myself from Upton Manor and must remain hidden until next July when my trust funds shall be returned to me.

'My governess, Miss Roberts, remained nearby after her dismissal and helped me with this scheme. In fact, sir, she was supposed to move into a vacant property on the Green, but when I went down there this morning, I discovered someone else was living there, and that she had cancelled her reservation.'

Cassie had pushed these worries to the back of her mind during the day, more concerned with the excitement of dining with her employer, but now she was telling him about it, her fears resurfaced.

'I am most concerned, sir, something untoward may have occurred. I can see no other reason why Miss Roberts should not now be living in the village; the only explanation I can come up with is that my uncle has detained her against her will.'

'It is a shocking story, Miss Forsythe. Although I could wish that you had not deceived me, in every other respect you're exactly as you said you were, and more than capable of caring for my daughter and of giving her the love and support she needs.'

Cassie's eyes rounded. 'Are you saying that you shall not throw me out of your house? That I may stay as your daughter's governess until next year?'

He leant forward, a strange glitter in his eyes. 'Do you think me so black-hearted, Miss Forsythe, that I should send you packing in the middle of a blizzard?'

She half smiled. 'Of course not, sir, but am I to stay on when the weather moderates?'

'You may, but I think it best if no one else knows your secret. It is one thing having a governess living here unchaperoned, but quite another a young lady of substance. Your reputation would be in tatters if it should become known.'

This was one aspect of the arrangement that neither she nor Ann had considered. 'That is of no matter, sir, as I have no intention of entering the marriage mart. For as soon as I am of age I shall buy an estate and live there with Miss Roberts. Why do I need a husband?'

'Do you have no wish for children of your own? It's a lonely life living as a spinster.'

'I should rather do that, sir, than live fighting like cat and dog as my parents did. It was a love match, not an arranged marriage, but they were never happy together — my father was jealous and my mother more so.'

The rattle of the tea trolley arriving prevented him from giving an answer. The parlour maid wheeled it in and left it, the copper urn gently steaming and hissing at Cassie's side. She was expected to make the tea and had no idea how to do it. She viewed it with disfavour.

'Do you wish to have tea, sir? I do not, and if you have no desire to have any either, then I shall not have to brave the vagaries of this contraption.'

He chuckled. 'Allow me to demonstrate, Miss Forsythe. If you care to watch the procedure, I'm sure that you shall have no difficulty performing this duty tomorrow night.'

Cassie felt a little thrill of pleasure at his casual assumption she would join him for dinner again. The tea made, he resumed his seat, his expression serious.

'As soon as the weather improves, Miss Forsyth, I shall make enquiries as to the whereabouts of your friend, Miss Roberts. I'm of the same opinion as you, it is likely that your uncle has detained her. Does she know your destination?' He frowned. 'Of course she does, how stupid of me to ask that. I'm afraid that Sir John might be exerting pressure on her to reveal where you are. Do you think Miss Roberts will buckle?'

Cassie shook her head vigorously. 'Never, she knows how important it is that I remain incognito. She is a resourceful woman, I'm sure she will prevail on my uncle to release her. It is my cousin that I'm worried about. Neither Ann, nor myself, can bear to see him suffer.'

'In that case, my dear, I shall extricate your Miss Roberts from Upton Manor as soon as may be.' He smiled as something occurred to him. 'In fact, I shall bring her here directly. Then she may take over your duties and become your chaperone and companion. That way everything will be as it should.'

Cassie excused herself soon after this, her head whirling with conflicting thoughts. The uppermost of which was, why should Mr Anderson wish to have a complete stranger living under his roof? If Ann became Amanda's governess then her presence would be redundant. What possible reason could he have for wishing her to stay at Martlesham Hall?

6

Cassie stumbled out of bed, eyes dark from lack of sleep. Events were moving out of her control, her life was being taken over in a quite unexpected way. She had had no choice but to tell her employer her secret. Why had he been so sanguine about her perfidy? There was something decidedly unsettling about the whole business.

As usual she collected Amanda and they went downstairs to eat together in the breakfast parlour. However, this morning she was disconcerted to find the room already occupied. Amanda ran forward in delight. 'Good morning, Papa, are you going to have breakfast with us today?'

'I am, my dear, it's something I do not do nearly often enough.'

Cassie nodded a greeting and half smiled, raising a quizzical eyebrow. She saw the gleam of humour in his eyes and she knew that his sudden appearance had nothing to do with his daughter and everything to do with seeing her.

She had become accustomed to her own routine at breakfast; Amanda and she took it in turns to serve each other.

'What would you like this morning, Miss Roberts?' The girl lifted the lids of the chafing dishes and standing on tip-toes to peer in. 'There are coddled eggs, ham slices, and I don't know what the other thing is, and field mushrooms. There is also toasted bread, hot rolls and conserve.'

'Let me think, Miss Amanda — this morning I shall have coddled eggs and toasted bread please. And if there is butter, then I should like a little of that as well.'

The parlour maid hurried in bringing the customary jug of chocolate which the girl placed beside Cassie. The whole time she was aware that she was under scrutiny from the man sitting at the far end of the table, his food congealing on his plate. Eventually Amanda had served herself as well and was safely seated, a napkin tucked in the neck of her pinafore.

'Shall I say grace, Miss Roberts?'

'I think this morning we shall miss that out, thank you, Miss Amanda.' Cassie could feel the disapproval radiating down the table. For some reason Mr Anderson did not approve of the Church, indeed did not seem to wish to even hear God's name mentioned in his house. What could have happened to destroy his faith?

The child, unaware of the tension, chattered on about this and that, being reminded gently not to talk with her mouth full. Cassie was only able to push the food around her plate, anything she put in her mouth felt as if she was chewing sawdust. Why did the wretched man not finish his meal and leave them in peace?

When Amanda had completed her meal her father was still sitting at the

93

table. Amanda looked first at him and then at Cassie. 'May I be excused, Papa, Miss Roberts? I still have a lesson to prepare that I didn't finish last night.'

Cassie waited for him to answer and when he didn't she said quickly, 'Yes, my dear, run along. I shall be with you directly.'

The door closed behind her charge, leaving them alone for the first time since the revelations of the previous night. She put her cutlery back on the table with a decided snap. 'Mr Anderson, why are you here? You never felt the need to breakfast with us before, it is most uncomfortable having you in here like this.'

He raised his hands and carefully dabbed his lips with his napkin before answering. 'Pray, excuse me if I'm incorrect, that I believe this is my home, and I am at liberty to eat where I wish?'

Cassie bit her tongue in annoyance. He was quite correct, of course, but she had not meant what he implied, and he knew that very well.

'Mr Anderson, things are difficult enough between us, now that you know how things are, can't you understand that having you here calling me by a name that is not mine, in front of your daughter, makes me uncomfortable?'

Immediately he stood up and walked round to her side. 'I had forgotten, Miss Roberts. I had not considered that aspect of things. It is against your nature to prevaricate in any way, is it not? The sooner the real Miss Roberts arrives and this charade can be put to rest, the better I shall like it.'

He turned away abruptly and strode to the window, scowling out at the snow as if it had fallen deliberately to annoy him. 'There's nothing I can do about it until the snow clears and heaven knows when that shall be. I have estate business to attend to, I shall not be around during the day, and fully understand if you prefer not to dine with me as things are.'

Cassie felt a rush of relief. 'Thank

you, sir. I have thought of a compromise, if you would consider it? Perhaps we could dine together, a little earlier, and invite Miss Amanda to join us?'

He hesitated for a moment before nodding. 'Very well, we shall do so tonight, but I do not intend to make habit of having a nursery tea.'

Cassie curtsied politely and hurried out before her wayward tongue said more than was wise. She prided herself on being level-headed, slow to anger and never speaking without thought, but these past few hours she had been behaving quite out of character. It was decidedly odd.

★ ★ ★

The next few days passed pleasantly enough. The three of them only dined together the once, and after that Cassie asked to have a tray sent up. She assumed Mr Anderson ate on his own in the dining room. She knew it would be foolish to spend any time alone with him as, for some reason, when in his vicinity her emotions were heightened and her tongue, and common sense, assumed a will of their own.

Four days after the blizzard she was awake before Molly arrived; she was finding it difficult to sleep at the moment. She went to the window, pulled back the heavy curtains and pushed open the shutters. She gaped at the scene in front of her. Overnight the snow had vanished; there was not a trace of it, apart from the snowman she and Amanda had built standing lonely in the middle of the park.

Mr Anderson could leave for Upton Manor and collect Ann. Cassie was becoming increasingly unhappy impersonating her friend; every time Amanda called her Miss Roberts she flinched. She wished she could explain to the child who she really was. But until Ann was safely away from Upton she had to hold her peace.

When she called for Amanda, her nanny opened the door. 'I'm sorry,

Miss Roberts, but Miss Amanda is a trifle poorly this morning and I've decided she'd be better staying in bed.'

'I do hope it's nothing serious, Nanny? Has she caught a chill from playing in the snow?'

'No, Miss Roberts, I think it was eating too much of cook's plum cake last night before supper, it has upset her stomach. A quiet day in bed will soon put her right again.'

'Good, give her my love, and I shall see her as usual tomorrow.'

Cassie realized that she had a day to herself, no duties to perform, no lessons to take, and knew immediately what she wished to do with her unexpected free time. She would enquire about borrowing a horse, it was long time since she'd ridden, but she thought it was a skill one never forgot. She was walking though the entrance hall as her employer was about to leave the house.

'Good morning Miss Roberts, I was about to send for you. I shall be leaving for Kent to collect your friend as soon as I return from some important estate business. The sudden thaw has caused flooding in some of the cottages and they are in need of urgent repair. I wish to see for myself what needs doing.'

'You are a conscientious landlord, Mr Anderson. Before you set off, I have a favour to ask. Is there a quiet horse that I might borrow? Your daughter has a stomach upset, nothing serious I can assure you, but I am free of my duties today and rather thought I might try my hand at riding again.'

'Yes, there is a mare that is used to pull the gig sometimes, but she also goes smoothly under sidesaddle. I shall ask Ned to saddle her up for you and be ready to accompany you when you come down.'

Cassie raced back upstairs unaware she showed an expanse of trim ankle that was most unseemly. She burst into her bedchamber where Molly was talking to the chambermaid.

'Molly, I am to go riding. It is a good thing that I thought to bring a habit with me. Can you help me change, I do not wish to keep the horses waiting in this weather.'

She arrived at the stables to find a small chestnut mare standing placidly, her reins looped over the arm of a smiling groom. 'Good morning, Miss Roberts. The master says I am to accompany you wherever you wish to go. You'll not come to any harm on Bess here, she's as quiet and gentle as a lamb.'

Cassie took the reins and turned to allow him to toss her up in to the saddle. She placed her knee around the pommel and rammed her other foot home in the stirrup iron. Then she carefully adjusted the skirts of her habit and was ready to go. As they clattered out on to the gravel circle in front of the house a young footman ran down the steps waving a letter.

'Miss Roberts, this note has just arrived from the village, the boy said that it was urgent.' Cassie frowned. Why should anyone be sending her a note, she knew no one living there? Then she smiled, she knew who it was from — Ann had arrived and, finding her cottage occupied, was contacting her for advice.

She urged her mare across to the footman and leant down to the take the note. It was folded and sealed with a blob of plain red wax. She dropped her reins, twisting them round her knee, sure the animal would remain still whilst she perused her letter. She recognised the handwriting immediately.

My dear friend,

As you have no doubt guessed, I am now in the village and waiting to meet you. I'm staying at the inn, I have taken rooms there for the present. Please come and see me as soon as you may, I have urgent news for you from Upton Manor.

My very best wishes,
Ann

Cassie read the note again, there was something slightly odd about it, something she could not quite put her finger on, it seemed a trifle stilted. She smiled and folded it up — never mind that — she could ask Ann herself when they met. She leant down and gave the piece of paper back to the waiting footman.

'Could you give that to Mr Anderson when he returns? It is very important that he reads it at once. Please tell him that I am going into the village, he will understand.'

The footman turned and hurried back inside, glad to get out of the cold wind; the temperature had risen by several degrees, but the biting east wind blowing straight from the North Sea was still whistling across the fields.

'I'm only riding to the village, Ned, I really don't think there's any need for you to accompany me, whatever Mr Anderson said. I shall go through Home Wood, you may come with me as far as that in order to open the gate. All I have to do is complete the mile to the village along a straight path and that will take me no more than fifteen minutes. I am visiting a friend who's staying at The Black Sheep, I do not wish anyone to be obliged to wait outside in the cold whilst I'm there.'

The young man looked uncertain, then nodded. 'If you're sure, miss, I shall come with you to the gate as you suggest. What time do you think you'll be returning?'

'I shall not be above an hour, so if you come back to open the gate at 11 o'clock, you should see me riding across the field.'

Cassie soon found her old expertise came back to her, indeed, the mare was a trifle sluggish for her taste, but ideal for a first venture. When they reached the exit from Home Woods, Ned dismounted and opened the gate for her.

'The field's a mite muddy, miss, so I should take it steady.'

'I've no intention of galloping today; it is many years since I've been on board a horse, I know my limitations.'

She heard the gate clunk shut behind her and urged her mount into a smooth trot. The path she was following was only visible from the gate at first, then it dipped and ran through a small coppice, over a stream and continued for another few hundred yards until it came to the outskirts of the village.

The sun was out, although with no heat, and it was shining directly into her eyes. Cassie was forced to screw them up in order to see ahead, whilst still watching the track for potholes and other imperfections. The last thing she wanted was a fall. Mr Anderson might refuse to lend her a mount next time she asked.

She didn't see the figures lurking in the trees beside the path so when a horse suddenly appeared in front of her she barely had time to rein back. Bess threw her head up in a panic and tried to back away, but a second roughly-dressed man appeared and grabbed the bit. Before Cassie could open her mouth to protest her attacker jumped forward. The next thing she knew her foot had been snatched from the stirrup and she was tumbling sideways to the ground. Her head crashed heavily on a stone at the side of the track and everything went black.

★ ★ ★

Jonathan Anderson cantered back to Martlesham Hall, his head full of the problems his tenants were facing, and ways in which he could help them. He had arranged for the cottagers whose homes were damaged to move in to the empty rooms behind the stables. It was not ideal, but they were warm and dry, and they could manage until the repairs were put in hand.

He vaulted from the saddle and tossed his reins to the waiting groom. He was about to turn away when he swung back, his face dark. 'What the hell are you doing here, Ned? You were told to accompany Miss Roberts on her ride.'

Ned blanched. 'Miss Roberts has only ridden into the village, sir. I accompanied her as far as the gate, and am to return to meet her thirty minutes from now.'

'I gave you instructions and expect them to be followed to the letter. I employ you, not Miss Roberts, unless you wish to seek work elsewhere?'

The young man mumbled a response and hung his head, wishing he was anywhere but there. Jonathan strode back to the house. He had some letters to write before he could leave, but decided he would wait until Cassie returned. As he tossed his riding coat, hat and gloves to the waiting footman the butler appeared, a silver salver in his hand, upon which was a note.

'Miss Roberts asked expressly for you to read this note, sir, as soon as you returned. She also asked me to inform you that she has ridden down to the village.'

'Thank you, Foster.' He took the piece of paper and scanned its contents.

Good God! This was excellent news, the missing Miss Roberts had arrived in Martlesham and was staying at The Black Sheep; this meant he wouldn't have to travel to Kent after all. It also meant that the young woman who was masquerading as a governess could reveal her true self and he could reveal his true feelings. Smiling he turned to Foster.

'I shall be going out again directly, hand me back my outer garments.'

Pushing the paper into his waistcoat pocket, he shrugged back into his riding coat and, jamming his beaver on his head, he ran back outside, taking the steps in one bound. Ten minutes later he was astride his horse, Bruno, and cantering through the wood; he didn't bother to open the five barred gate, he jumped it.

He clattered into the inn and dismounting, tossed his reins to a waiting ostler. He strode into the inn, to be met by the landlord.

'Good morning, sir, this is an

unexpected pleasure. Can I be of assistance?'

'I have come to escort Miss Roberts home, she's visiting a friend who's staying on your premises.'

The man scratched his head. 'I fear you're mistaken, sir, we have no one staying with us at present, and I've not seen Miss Roberts at all today.'

Jonathan felt a cold dread to sweep over him. Something had happened to Cassie. She had left Home Wood just over thirty minutes ago. He had not passed her, had seen no sign of her, so where the hell was she?

He forced a smile to his face, no need to worry the innkeeper or start rumours flashing around the village. 'I must've been mistaken, landlord, thank you for your time.'

He leapt down the steps and into the stable yard and, snatching the reins from the ostler, he vaulted back into the saddle and pushed the stallion into a gallop, scattering unwary pedestrians in all directions.

He thundered down the High Street, his dramatic passage sending villagers scurrying for safety. So much for wishing to keep matters quiet, he thought ruefully as he jumped back onto the path. He reined in, looking carefully at the way ahead. There was only one place Cassie could have been waylaid, he decided — at the coppice.

Pushing his horse back into a gallop he raced to the wood. He reined back so sharply the animal was forced back on his hind quarters and almost fell. He jumped down and pulling the reins over the animal's head shouted, 'Stay where you are, Bruno.'

He looked around for signs of a recent disturbance. As he had just galloped through, in both directions, it was hard at first tell how many other horses had been this way. Bruno's large feet were easily recognized, and then he spotted the small and more dainty shape of the mare. He drooped to his knees and next to them were the definite imprint of men's boots and of another horse. Then he saw something that made his blood run cold.

There was a large stone at the side of the path and as he knelt in the mud he could see quite clearly see the stain of blood, next to it was a dent that could only have been made by a falling body.

Cassie had been abducted, and on the evidence he had before him, she was sorely injured. His eyes narrowed in fury. Whoever had perpetrated this evil deed would not live to speak about it, not if he had his way.

7

Cassie regained consciousness to find herself inside a moving carriage. Her hands were tied behind her back but her feet were still free beneath her skirt. She had lost her hat and her hair was escaping from the bun she'd worn at the nape of her neck. She lay with eyes closed, trying to organise her thoughts. If only her head did not hurt so abominably

She recalled being accosted on the path to the village and then a rough man tipping her out of the saddle, after that a searing pain on her temple and then nothing. The vehicle she was travelling in was moving faster than was wise in the weather conditions. Every few minutes it lurched and bumped as it hit a rut or pothole in the road. She doubted if they were using the toll route, more likely a back lane where the coach wouldn't be seen, which would account for their unstable progress.

Of one thing she was certain — her incarceration had been the work of Sir John. Somehow he had persuaded Ann to write the letter that drew her out of the house and allowed his men to abduct her. She was about to attempt to sit up and demand to have to her hands released when something awful occurred to her. She had supposed that Sir John was having her transported back to Upton Manor in order to force her to marry her cousin. Now she understood she was wrong — if she died, he was her only surviving relative and would inherit her fortune.

Although it was her aunt who was her blood relative, by law everything belonged to her husband. She had never believed he could stoop to murder. Was he so desperate for money that he would risk his own life to obtain it?

The way she had been treated, tied up and tossed on to the floor, made her believe she was not intended to survive the ordeal. These men were evil villains, taking her somewhere lonely where she could be dispatched and buried and no one the wiser.

Her head hurt, making it difficult to think, to plan how she might escape when the men were least expecting it. If she lay still they would think her still unconscious; her legs were free so when they tried to move her from the coach, that might be her opportunity. She would lash out, and if God was with her, she would be able to run and hide until help arrived.

Cassie had little knowledge of the area she had been living in these past weeks, but she was aware it was about an hour's ride from Martlesham Hall to the bleak Suffolk coast, an area frequented mainly by smugglers and occasionally by intrepid fishermen. She knew that must be where they were heading, it was the obvious place to dispose of an unwanted female. They wouldn't even have to kill her, merely throw her into the sea and the water would do the rest.

This time of year she was certain the temperature of the sea was so low it would kill her long before she drowned. Then her uncle could claim innocence and her death be considered a tragic accident. Of course they would have to untie her arms before they threw her in — would that be her best chance of escape? How had things come to this? Her life had been miserable since her parents died, but she had never felt herself to be in any danger; now she knew she was fighting to stay alive.

The smell of the man sitting inside her made her gag, his rank breath and unwashed body permeated the air. He would not hesitate to knock her unconscious again if she made the slightest move. She thought about the time just before she had been taken, had she not told the young groom to meet her after one hour at the large five barred gate that led out from Home Woods? If he had done so and she didn't appear, surely he would have raised the alarm by now? A flash of hope made her pulse jump as something significant occurred to her.

Mr Anderson was intending to return to the Hall before he set off for Kent to rescue Ann. He would see the note she had left and receive her message. She was sure he would check at The Black Sheep, discover there was no one staying there and understand that something dire had taken place. He would come in search of her, he would not let her be carried away by these rough men.

For a few moments she rejoiced in her imminent rescue, then her spirits sank to their lowest point. How would he know which direction they'd taken? He would be expecting her to be returned to Kent, would never for a moment suspect that her uncle might wish to dispose of her permanently, that he had abandoned any hope of persuading her to marry his son and intended to gain access to her inheritance in the cruellest way.

The rocking and bumping was beginning to make her feel nauseous and she feared she would be sick and then be obliged to lie in the mess she'd made. The very thought of having to do that settled her stomach. Suddenly the carriage lurched more alarmingly, there was an ominous cracking and her world turned over and over. For a second time that morning she lost her senses as her head hit the side of the upturned carriage.

* ★ ★

Jonathan galloped back to Martlesham Hall, shouting to attract attention as he arrived in a skid of gravel. Within minutes he had explained to his valet, Samuel, and his estate manager, Peter Hodgkin, what he wanted them to do for him. He ran inside and snatched up his duelling pistols, also pushing a thin stiletto down the side of his right boot. It was wise to be prepared. He sent a groom galloping to Ipswich to raise the

116

militia, and then with four men, all armed with pistols and cudgels, galloped back down the drive and through the woods.

All this had taken him less than one quarter of an hour to arrange. He had also had time to dash off a quick note to be taken post-haste to a friend in London, who was a member of the government. In it he asked for a Bow Street runner and some constables to be sent down to Upton Manor in Kent to arrest Digby and rescue the real Miss Roberts.

Satisfied he had done everything he could, he concentrated on his urgent mission to recover Miss Forsythe. He told the group to dismount ten yards from where the abduction had taken place.

'I want to see which way they went, I didn't stop to look when I was here a little while ago. The ground is muddy, it should be easy to pick up their tracks. There was certainly one horse and two men possibly more.'

Samuel remained where he was, holding the reins of the five horses as the others, keeping to the grassy areas on either side of the path, headed for the coppice.

When he saw the bloodstained stone for the second time Jonathan's rage increased. He had only known this softly spoken, beautiful girl for a few weeks, but already he was certain he had finally found the woman he had been waiting for all his life. At last he could put behind him the misery of his first marriage and begin again.

Tom, the head coachman, called out to him. 'Sir, over here, I've found their tracks. I'm sure there were only two of them, but both mounted.'

Jonathan ran over to see what the man had found. He dropped to his knees, ignoring the dirt, and stared at the imprints. Yes, there were definitely two sets of horses' hoofs and two different imprints made by down-at-heel boots.

'Look, sir, the prints of this horse are

deeper than they were on the far side of the track, I think one of them must have been carrying Miss Roberts.'

Jonathan straightened and shouting for the horses to be brought up turned to the three men and gave them their orders. 'Tom, you lead, let's see if we can follow these villains back through the fields. There's scarcely a path at all, more a rabbit track than anything else. The hoof prints should be clearly visible, one will have been leading Bess.'

Remounted he set off close behind, they arrived at an open gate and outside he saw the wheel marks from a carriage.

'Dammit, they have transferred her to a coach. That means there must be more than two of them, at least three by my reckoning. Which way do you think they went, Tom? They will be heading for Kent, but I doubt they'll want to take the toll road to Colchester, they'll have to go by back lanes to avoid being seen.'

Tom was examining the wheel marks, a puzzled expression on his face. 'I don't think they're heading south, sir, it looks like they've turned the carriage and are going straight towards the coast.'

Jonathan stared at him for a moment unable to think of a logical explanation. It did not take him long to reach the conclusion that Sir John must want her money so badly he was prepared to murder in order to obtain it. The man must be her sole heir and would stand to inherit everything if she was to die unexpectedly. Drowning would be the perfect way, and no suspicion could fall on him if the event took place so far from his home. It would be deemed a tragic accident, and he would have achieved his objective far more easily than if he had continued to coerce a reluctant bride to the altar and then steal her money. His blood ran cold as he understood the importance of this.

'Good God! This is not an abduction, it is a murder attempt. We must ride flat out, Miss Roberts' very life depends on us arriving at the coast before they do.'

They raced pell-mell across the bleak countryside and had travelled several miles, Jonathan keeping one eye out for the wheel marks and hoof prints, the other on the road ahead when, from the superior height of his stallion, he saw over the hedge something in the lane half a mile ahead. Slewed across the track was a carriage, its wheels still spinning in the air.

Instantly he reined back, wrenching his horse's head around to block the road and stop the other four from continuing their wild ride and revealing their presence. In the resulting mêlée one of the grooms, Ned, was thrown into a deep water-filled ditch that ran alongside the hedge. Tom vaulted from his saddle and hauled his friend back out. They were none the worse for their ducking, but Jonathan feared the noise they'd made could have alerted the men barely half a mile ahead.

He dismounted, tossing his reins to

the dripping groom, and shinned expertly up a convenient tree. Although it was leafless there was enough ivy twining amongst the branches to give him the camouflage he required. He looked carefully along the lane in the direction of the tilted carriage. It was clear that the rear axle had broken. He waved his hand and put his finger to his lips, indicating the rest of his party should remain silent so that he could listen.

Thank God he'd seen the carriage before they'd rounded the bend. He smiled grimly. He had been calling on his Maker rather a lot lately — was he finally getting over his lack of belief? Had meeting a lovely young girl restored his faith in God?

He strained his ears and could just hear the noise of one man shouting, the stamping of horses and jangling of harnesses, but nothing else. He dropped from the tree and drew his pistols, loading and priming them before tucking them into his belt. He watched his companions do the same. Cudgels were unstrapped from their places behind sandals, and then they were ready. He beckoned and they moved in closer.

'We must approach on foot. Tom, you and Ned go through the hedge and creep along the side — try not to fall in the ditch again! Sam, you and Jim go through and approach from the far side of the lane. I shall ride directly to them. With any luck they will mistake me for a passing squire and allow me the time I need to get close enough to shoot.'

He turned and mounted his stallion. He hoped his scheme would give his men time to be in shooting range as well. He kicked Bruno forward and as soon as he was in hailing distance he called out loudly. 'Good day to you — can I be of some assistance? I do hope nobody has been injured in the accident?'

There was only one man visible, an evil-looking fellow dressed in rough clothes and with a mouthful of black and broken teeth. The man scowled, making a rude gesture in his direction.

'We don't need you — clear off. What's going on here is none of your business.'

Jonathan looked round frantically. Where the hell was Miss Forsythe? Then with a sickening lurch in his stomach he saw that the carriage was partially submerged in the water of the same ditch that Ned had fallen into.

Forgetting he was supposed to be an innocent bystander he jammed his heels into Bruno's side and, drawing his pistol, fired directly at the man — killing him stone dead. He didn't wait to see him fall, just threw himself from the saddle, shouting for his men to come and assist him.

Somehow he scrambled up the side of the coach and pulled the door open. For a moment he could see nothing, then in a tumbled heap he saw two bodies, one Miss Forsythe, the other a man. Had his wild ride been in vain? Was he too late to save his love?

8

Jonathan didn't wait for his men to arrive, just tipped himself headfirst into the interior of the coach. He fell into the darkness, managing to stop his fall before he crushed the young woman half submerged in the freezing water that had entered the coach.

Frantically he scrabbled and, grasping two handfuls of her dress, heaved her up. He couldn't tell if she was alive or dead, all he knew was that she was limp and unresponsive. He ignored the body of the rank-smelling man — if he was dead, it was no more than he deserved. He righted the limp shape until her head was against his shoulder. He felt under her chin for a pulse and thought he detected a steady beat, but he couldn't be sure; his hands were shaking so much it could be him that was moving and not the corpse-like girl

125

he held in his arms. Where the hell were his men?

He roared for assistance and he felt the vehicle rock as Ned's head appeared in the square of sky above him. 'Hang on a minute, sir, Tom has a rope round his waist and is just unwinding it. We'll have you out of there in a jiffy.'

Ned's face disappeared and seconds later a rope snaked in, the end dropping beside him. He quickly wrapped it round his wrist and grasping it firmly before shouting to his men, 'Right, haul away, but remember there's two of us so you'll have to brace yourselves.'

Inch by painful inch he was pulled upwards, his arm feeling as if it was tearing from his shoulder socket. Initially he was able to use his feet, first against the sides of the coach and then the roof, to assist them, but at the end he was swinging free, supporting all the weight with his one arm.

Hands reached in and he was heaved to safety and his precious burden taken from him. He fell headlong, barely getting his arms down in time to break his fall, his injured shoulder protesting at the brutal treatment. He didn't care about that, he had more pressing concerns — whether his beloved lived or died.

'Give Miss Roberts to me. Wait, my coat is wet, I need a dry one.' Jim removed his riding cape and covered him with it before placing Cassandra in his arms. Jonathan walked away from the carriage and waited for Jim to spread his coat on the ground, and only then did he release his burden. He saw she had massive bruise on her temple and a gaping cut, and realised that his shoulder, upon which her head had rested, was darkened by her blood.

He reached round behind her face and his fingers came away red and sticky. He lowered his ear to her lips, and to his profound relief he felt the gentle expiration of breath. She was deeply unconscious, but by some miracle not drowned as he had feared. He didn't understand how she could have been submerged head first in the water for so long and not be dead. Closing his eyes, he thanked God for the second time in several years, and meant it.

He knew that time was not on their side. There were only a couple of hours of daylight left, and he had to get her back to Martlesham Hall and get the physician to attend to her injuries. He wrapped her tight in the warm dry coat and scooped her up, wincing as his shoulder protested. He turned to survey the wreck of the coach.

'I'm sure there were three men. Has anyone seen the third?' He knew two of the villains were dead, but he didn't want to be shot at by the remaining one. Tom had been busy cutting free the terrified horses whilst Jim had been looking around for Bruno. It was his voice that called back the information he needed.

'There's a corpse over here, sir, it looks like he was thrown from the coach and broke his neck. Bloody good job I'd say.'

Jonathan echoed those sentiments. 'Good. I need to get Miss Roberts back home as quickly as I can. Jim, come over here.' He handed his precious girl over whilst he mounted. He then leant down to take her and settled her across the pommel.

'Jim, I need you to stay here, and wait for the militia to arrive. They should be on their way before dark.' He realised that he had this man's warm coat around Miss Forsythe; the young man would freeze left out here without protection. Jonathan groped in his jacket pocket and removed a tinderbox. 'Here, lad, take this. I'll be home in half an hour, you'll be standing out here for a while yet. Gather some wood, use the coach if you can't find any. and make yourself a fire. I reckon you'll need one before this night's done.'

While Jonathan headed for home, Sam went galloping for Dr Fisher. Jonathan prayed the man wasn't out attending a difficult birth or death and unable to come. He couldn't gallop his stallion with a double weight, but the horse had a smooth canter and at this pace the miles were soon covered and hardly more than two hours after he'd first left his home he returned with Cassie in his arms.

The doctor arrived and was sent straight up to attend to Miss Forsythe. He was thinking of her by her given name now, Cassie. It was a strange name, Cassandra, but it suited her better than Ann. He knew that her abigail, and the chambermaid, had stripped away her soaked garments and replaced them with a thick flannelette nightgown. Next she had been wrapped in red flannel and hot bricks had been placed all around her. By the time the doctor had arrived her temperature had begun to rise and he no longer feared she would die from the cold. However, he was deeply concerned by her continuing lack of consciousness.

When the doctor emerged from her bedchamber Jonathan was waiting anxiously, his back to the roaring fire, in her sitting room.

'I have stitched both her wounds. They looked more serious than they were. However, until she recovers consciousness I cannot say if there has been permanent damage done to her brain. The longer she is like this the greater the danger of her not making a full recovery'

'But she's in no danger at this moment?'

'No, Mr Anderson, her condition is serious, but stable.'

'I cannot understand how she wasn't drowned, she must have been under-water for several minutes and yet still she lives. I believe it was a miracle.'

'It could well have been, sir, but I have seen cases like this before. When a person enters the water already uncon-scious they inhale little water and often survive submersion, where others who fall in fully awake, perish.' The man smiled reassuringly. 'Also, the shock of the cold water would have slowed her breathing even more; it was the combination of the two that, in my opinion, saved her life.'

Jonathan didn't care what the scientific explanation was, he knew there had been divine intervention. He had turned back to God, and his prayers were now being answered.

'I thank you, sir. Shall you be calling again today?'

'I think not. My patient is comfortable, but never fear I shall be back first thing tomorrow morning to see how she does.'

Jonathan had to be content with that. He accompanied the doctor downstairs, thanking him for his prompt attendance and diagnosis. He glanced out of the window, seeing it was now dark. Peter Hodgkin, his estate manager, had waylaid the militia and taken them straight to the ruined coach. No doubt the man in charge would return wanting an explanation, but he doubted it would be tonight. He hoped the fact that he'd shot one through the heart would not brand him a murderer.

He had explained to his daughter what had happened, told her that her dear Miss Roberts was in fact one Miss Cassandra Forsythe and the real Miss Roberts would be on her way to take up her duties soon. He had expected Amanda to be desolate at the loss of her governess, but for some reason she'd taken the news with equanimity and smiled as if at a secret joke.

'As long as Miss Forsythe is still going to be living here, I shall not mind having a different governess. I'm sure that the real Miss Roberts must be a kind and understanding teacher, or she would not be the closest friend of our Miss Forsythe.'

'I'm sure you're right, my love. Dr Fisher has said you cannot visit at the moment, and neither can I, but her abigail will keep us informed of any changes. I'm sure she'll make a full recovery and come back to us very soon.'

His daughter ran forward and gave him an impulsive hug. He stiffened — he did not usually encourage such physical contact — but found he actually enjoyed the embrace. With gentle hands he enfolded her against him, lifting her from her feet so that her legs dangled free. 'Life will improve now, my darling girl, and we shall all be happy again, I promise you.'

'I shall always miss my mama, but she would not want us to grieve for her any longer. She would want us both to find a new life and be happy, wouldn't she, Papa?'

He closed his eyes and felt the familiar pain of shattered hopes and trampled dreams, but somehow he recovered. 'Of course she would, my dear girl. Now run along to your nanny, I'm sure she can find you something with which to occupy your time.'

'I'm going to the schoolroom, I intend to paint a picture for Miss

Forsythe. Shall I bring it down for you to see when it's finished, Papa?'

'Do that, my dear.' He watched the pretty fair-haired child skip happily from the drawing room and for the first time since his wife died he began to feel that he might be getting over that dark period.

★ ★ ★

Cassie woke the following morning to find herself safely in her bed. Her head was bandaged and hurt if she moved it so much as an inch. She didn't know what had transpired, only that she must have been in an accident of some sort and Mr Anderson had rescued her. She sent up a heartfelt prayer thanking God for his intervention. She prayed that her dear friend, Ann, would soon be with her, and then she knew she would start to feel better.

She drifted in and out of wakefulness over the next few days, sitting up to swallow a few mouthfuls of broth or

135

lemonade then falling back into semi-consciousness. For some reason she didn't seem to have the strength to wake up completely, as if something was holding her back, something so awful she couldn't bear to face it. She had no recollection of her abduction or near drowning, her mind was mercifully blank for the moment.

A week after her accident she opened her eyes to see Ann sitting by the bed, her sweet face smiling down at her. 'My dear, you have had us very worried, but I see that your eyes are finally clear. Can I assist you to sit? It is high time you ate something more substantial than a few mouthfuls of broth.'

For the first time since her injuries Cassie felt ready to face the world. 'Ann, I'm so glad to see you. Yes, do please help me up.' She paused, a look of urgency on her face. 'I need to use the commode, I do hope it's not far away or I shall disgrace myself.'

Comfortable, and back in bed, her head mercifully no longer spinning when she moved it and her memory quite lucid she wanted to hear all the news. 'Tell me, how did you come to write that letter? How did you get here? You must tell me everything, I'm desperate to know.' She nodded to encourage her and immediately wished that she had not. 'I remember now that Sir John arranged for me to be murdered, so there's no need to hedge around the facts.'

'I shall tell you everything later, my love, but first you must eat. I rang the bell as soon as I saw you stirring and Molly has run down to fetch you a tray.'

Cassie found she was hungry, and could have eaten more than the gently coddled eggs, weak tea and toasted bread that arrived. But Ann had told her it would not be a good idea to overfill her stomach when it had been empty for so long. She settled back on the pillows and waited to receive the two visitors that were insisting they came in to see her now she was awake.

Mr Anderson arrived, Amanda walking politely behind him. The smile he gave her warmed her heart, and she knew she had not been mistaken. He reciprocated her feelings.

'How are you, Miss Forsythe? Amanda and I have been beside ourselves with worry. But I can see that we need not have done so, as you're looking almost restored. With a few days of good food I'm sure you shall be back as you were.'

Amanda sidled close to the bed and shyly put her hand on the coverlet. Cassie opened her arms and the child needed no further bidding, she scrambled up and flung herself against Cassie's chest. As she hugged and soothed her, telling her she was a silly goose and should not have worried, it would take more than a bump on the head to do her in, she glanced up and saw a strange glitter in Mr Anderson's eyes. Could it be tears she saw there? Surely not, he was a man, he would not let emotions carry him away.

He had said little of note during the short visit, but she felt the power of his approval, saw something in his face that she believed was love. When he took his daughter away later she was exhausted but happy.

'I can see by your expression, Ann, that you see how things are with us. I found myself falling in love with him, and I believe that he returns my affections. We have not spoken of it, not really, but as soon as I'm well I'm sure something will be said.'

'I know I should not tell you this, my dear, but it's already been spoken of. Mr Anderson assured me his intentions are absolutely honourable, that the reason he wanted me here so promptly is to protect your reputation. It seems he has already spoken to the vicar, and has sent his estate manager to procure a special licence from London.'

Cassie was stunned. Events are moving far quicker than she thought decent. 'A special licence? Why should we require that? We've only been acquainted a few weeks, and now that you're here there can be no question that I'm unchaperoned. I had hoped we would have a few months to get to know each other better before we actually got married.'

'It seems, in the circumstances, that you are in need of a new guardian. Sir John is still legally the recipient of the interest from your trust fund, and in spite of being obliged to flee the country he can still live on your money until you are one and twenty. I think that Mr Anderson believes he would make a better administrator than Sir John ever did.'

Cassie closed her eyes to digest this information. She knew that Mr Anderson . . . she must start thinking of him as Jonathan she supposed . . . was a wealthy man and had no need of her inheritance, and he was quite right, it was immoral for that monster and his wife to benefit a moment longer.

'I suppose there is sense in what you say. But I must have a new wardrobe before I can marry — indeed before I can leave this room.' She giggled suddenly; she was being a trifle premature. 'Listen to me, I'm already marching us down the aisle and I have not yet received an offer.'

'The only reason he hasn't done so, my dear girl, is that you have been unconscious. As soon as you are able to sit on the *chaise-longue* in your sitting room, he will be there to speak to you.'

Two days later she was resting on the day bed in her parlour when Molly came in bringing a small, grey-haired woman with her. 'Miss Forsyth, this is the mantua maker, Madame Ducray, she has come to take your measurements. Look, she's brought with her fashion plates from *The Belle Assemblée* so you can choose gowns that are at the height of fashion.'

'Forgive me for intruding, Miss Forsyth, but Mr Anderson suggested that you might wish for some fresh gowns before you leave your rooms.'

Cassie smiled. How thoughtful of

Jonathan, to have had the same idea. Of course she didn't want to appear dressed in identical clothes to the real Miss Roberts. She must now take her proper place in the household and would need suitable garments in which to do so.

'You are very welcome, Madame Ducray, I should dearly love to replenish my wardrobe for I have nothing suitable to wear.'

She spent a happy hour selecting designs for morning dresses, tea dresses, walking dresses, riding habits, evening gowns and even a ball gown. There were to be pelisses, spencers and shawls to compliment each outfit. She also chose, gloves, slippers, reticules and fans to complete her extravagances.

As she was examining material samples Madame Ducray sighed loudly. 'We 'ave been so very 'appy that monsieur 'as found 'imself another bride. Mr Anderson 'as been so very down since the dreadful accident three years ago.'

Cassie had the opportunity she'd

longed for — she could finally get some answers to the things that puzzled her. 'How did Mrs Anderson die, Madame?'

'She fell from 'er 'orse and broke 'er neck. Poor Mr Anderson was obliged to fetch 'er back. Monsieur 'ad been out riding too and found 'is poor lady dead.'

'How sad. It's small wonder that Miss Anderson does not wish to ride any more. Her mother must have been fair, like her daughter, for Mr Anderson is both dark complexioned and haired.'

'Oh no! Mrs Anderson was as dark 'as 'er 'usband, Miss Forsythe. We 'ave always thought the little girl must take after 'er grandmother.'

'Well, it matters not, for she's a lovely girl and will grow up to be a beauty.' Cassie thought she had gossiped enough. 'Now, Madame Ducray, these are the fabrics that I wish to have.'

9

After the seamstress left Cassie settled back to read a novel feeling tired but content. Amanda was in the kitchen helping Cook make cakes for afternoon tea. Ann came in to visit her.

'You look tired, my dear. I don't think I shall stay long with you, you need to rest. Mr Anderson said he was coming to speak with you at four o'clock this afternoon.' Her friend smiled archly. 'And I'm sure you know very well the reason for his visit.'

'I believe so, but I hope that he's not coming to make me an offer. I learnt something whilst Madame was here that has only added to my unease about the mystery surrounding his first marriage and his wife's death.'

'Whatever do you mean? Tell me, what has the wretched woman told you?'

'Well, it seems that the first Mrs Anderson died in a riding accident, at least that's what everyone believes. Jonathan was out on estate business when his wife had her accident, he brought her home with her neck broken.'

Ann pursed her lips. 'I hope you're not suggesting that he had anything to do with her death? That is preposterous, my dear.'

'No more preposterous than the fact he shot one of my abductors in cold blood.' Cassie had learnt this piece of gossip from Molly, who told her it was the talk of the servant's hall. Everybody else seemed to think it made Mr Anderson a hero of some sort, but coupled with the information she'd just heard about the death of his first wife, it made her wonder if there was something he was hiding.

'I think that your recent injuries have made you worry unnecessarily. My advice is to forget all about it. Mr Anderson is a good man, and he loves you, there is no doubt about that. His distress whilst you were so ill made that perfectly clear. And Miss Amanda adores you too, she confided in me that she expects you to be her new mama and is delighted at the prospect.'

Cassie's head ached, she didn't want to think about it any more. She closed her eyes and laid back against the cushions. She thought she'd only closed her eyes for a moment, but when she opened them again the room was empty and the stream of sunlight that had been casting a pattern on the polished boards had moved. She must have been asleep for at least an hour.

She glanced at the mantel clock and saw that it was little after three. Good heavens! She must tidy herself up, Jonathan was coming to speak to her soon. She reached out and rang the little brass bell on the side table and Molly appeared immediately.

'Molly, can you assist me back to my chamber? I would like to put on something clean and perhaps you can dress my hair again?'

Her abigail hurried over and helped her from the daybed. She leant heavily on her maid's arm, her legs surprisingly wobbly. It took almost the whole hour for her to wash, change into a fresh gown and have her hair carefully arranged so that it no longer pulled on her sutures. It was ten minutes to four when she eventually returned to her sitting room.

'Your hair suits you hanging loose, Miss Cassie, it's such a rich red-brown. I'm certain there's not many ladies that have the natural waves you do.'

Cassie paused for a moment to glance at her reflection in one of the pier gilt mirrors that hung on either side of a window. 'I am far too pale, and even with my hair loose you can still see the bruising on my temple.' There was no use worrying about her appearance, if Jonathan still wished to marry her having seen her upside down in ditchwater, then she must look positively blooming now.

She was resettled, a patchwork quilt across her knees, when there was a soft tap at the door. Molly smiled knowingly and went across to open it. Good grief, did everyone know what was about to happen? Annoyance gave Cassie the strength to sit up straight, and added much-needed sparkle to her eyes.

As expected, her visitor was Jonathan — his hair, which he wore cut short in the modern style, well brushed, his dark blue jacket and silk waistcoat a perfect foil to the snowy cravat tied expertly beneath his chin. She didn't lower her eyes to see what colour his inexpressibles were, or if his boots were highly polished, that would be indelicate.

He stood at the door, a slight smile playing around his mouth, and half bowed. 'You are looking a deal better than you did when I visited yesterday. May I come in and speak to you?'

'Of course you can. I've been expecting you.'

Molly vanished with a whisk of

navy-blue skirts, leaving them alone. Cassie watched him pick up a heavy wooden chair in one hand and carry it as if it were no more than a basket of fruit. He placed it within arm's reach of her, then sat down and, folding his arms, stared directly at her.

She flushed under his gaze, revealing instantly that she knew the purpose of this afternoon visit. Instantly he grinned. 'Oh dear, I see you have been fore-warned. Shall I get down on one knee, or may I ask you sitting in a chair?'

She relaxed, her lips twitching. 'Well, sir, you must be on your knee, nothing else will satisfy me.'

With a chuckle he dropped and clasped her hands to his heart. 'Miss Forsythe, will you make me the happiest of men? Will you do me the inestimable honour of becoming my wife?'

She didn't hesitate. Since she'd met him her reservations about marriage had vanished like the snow. 'Of course I will. In fact, you already knew what my answer would be. Why else would you have come in here looking so smug?' It was not quite the reply he'd expected but it reduced the tension wonderfully. Instead of returning to his chair he leaned over and cupped her face. He gazed at her as if imprinting her image in his memory. Then, to her consternation he closed the few inches between them and she received her first adult kiss.

For a moment she froze — the feeling of a man's lips upon her own was so unexpected, so alien. Then a strange heat began to flood her limbs and her heart raced. Without conscious thought she swayed towards him, her fingers gripping his jacket and his kiss deepened.

A wonderful five minutes later he released her, his eyes dark with something she didn't understand. Breathless, transported to a place she hadn't known existed, she smiled at him tremulously, unable to say what was in her heart.

He raised her hand to his mouth and

kissed each finger tip, the heat of his lips sending shockwaves down her arms and her head spun. She heard him stand, and there was a faint rustling of clothes as he returned to his chair. Her heart began to return to its normal pace.

'Well, my darling, we are now affianced. As no doubt you've already been told, I have sent for a special license. Your uncle and your aunt have fled the country rather than face charges of attempted murder, but he's still your legal guardian until we are married. Only then will he no longer have access to your money.'

She smiled guiltily. 'As you no doubt suspected, sir, Miss Roberts had already told me that. I must apologise for her indiscretion, but you know how it is between bosom bows.'

'Actually, my dear, I don't. No doubt as time goes by I shall adapt to having no secrets in my own house.'

Cassie smiled, this was a perfect opportunity to ask him to explain about his first marriage, but she hesitated. Although she loved him, she didn't know him well. They had only been acquainted a few weeks, and the relationship between employer and governess was quite different to that of a betrothed couple.

'I have no objection to being married as soon as my trousseau is completed. I have the matter in hand, and am assured by the seamstress that I shall have it in its entirety within four weeks.'

He frowned. 'Four weeks! Good God, we have no need with special licence in that case, we could have the banns called at the local church. Surely you don't need more than one or two gowns in order to get wed?'

She laughed at his expression. 'Well, I suppose you're right. As we're marrying here, I don't require all my gowns to be completed. But I cannot go about in public — I must have my wardrobe ready before you introduce me as your wife.'

He grinned, a decided gleam in his

eye. 'Excellent. I have no intention of taking you around the countryside for a few weeks.' His smile was decidedly wolfish. 'There are more enjoyable pastimes we can explore together. Now all you have to do is get well. The doctor assures me you should be back on your feet by the end of the week. He's coming tomorrow to remove your stitches.'

He leant across and placing a finger under her chin tipped her head back the better to examine the row of neat black knots across her temple. 'Is it still very sore, my darling?'

She shook her head, glad she no longer felt the searing pain she had initially. 'No, the sutures pull a little, but apart from that it looks far worse than it feels.'

He pushed back his chair and stood up. 'I shall be away for a few days, I have to go to Norwich on business. I postponed this visit whilst you were so ill. Now you have Miss Roberts here to take care of you, I can go confident that you'll come to no harm in my absence.'

'I shall miss you . . . Jonathan. Take care, the roads are still treacherous.'

He smiled and she felt herself melting under his stare. 'From now on I shall take extra care, my love. I have finally got something to come home to.'

★ ★ ★

Two days later Cassie was up and about and feeling almost as sprightly as she had before her unpleasant experiences. She decided that if she was to be married the following week it was high time she saw what would be her new accommodation. She asked her friend to accompany her to the master suite.

She tried the handle of the room she assumed would be hers. 'The door's locked, shall I send down to the housekeeper for the keys, Ann?'

Ann shook her head. 'No, let's go through Mr Anderson's chambers, perhaps the communicating door will have the key in it.'

For a moment Cassie hesitated, feeling it would be an intrusion into his privacy to enter his rooms without permission. She was about to voice her disquiet, but her friend vanished, obviously having no such qualms. There was no option but to follow her.

She stood in the door looking round — the room seemed to be dominated by the huge tester bed, its hangings of fine gold brocade matching the window curtains. She felt herself blushing at the thought of what she would experience in that very bed in less than a week's time.

Hastily she pushed these thoughts from her head and ran after Ann who had already unlocked the communicating door and vanished for a second time. This door led into what had been the first Mrs Anderson's rooms. This also had a large bed, but it was smaller than Jonathan's, and the drapes were of a pretty damask satin. She looked around in astonishment. 'Goodness! Look at the layer of dust on everything.

It looks as though someone has just left, and is about to come back. See the bed has not been pulled up, and there are bottles spilled on the dressing table. I do believe it hasn't been touched since the day she died.'

Ann was standing at the escritoire reading a sheet of paper left lying carelessly on the desktop. Cassie went to join her, wondering why her friend hadn't answered. Ann attempted to conceal the paper, but she was too late. Cassie saw it was a letter; as she scanned the words her blood ran cold and all her happiness drained away.

My darling Robert,

It is over. The truth has come out. When he discovered that I am once more with child he knew at once that it couldn't be his baby I am carrying. We have not laid together as man and wife for months. He has gone out riding. He left in a terrible rage, I fear for my life when he returns.

I could not help myself, my love, I

blurted out the whole — that my darling Amanda is your daughter, not his. That we have been lovers since I returned from honeymoon. I told him that I had been forced to marry him, that my parents considered a vicar too far beneath me to be my husband, and that they needed a substantial settlement in order to clear my brother's gambling debts.

I know we were wrong to play him false, Jonathan is a good man, he truly loved me, and has always done his best.

Here the page was splattered with what could only be tears, the ink smudged and the words hard to read. Cassie took the paper over to the window in order to see it more clearly. She tilted the paper towards the sunlight and she was able to just make out the rest of the letter.

I cannot stay here any longer, he will reject us both. I am going to pack our things and order the carriage, then we shall come to you. I have no idea how we shall manage. The scandal will be impossible, but I can no longer stay here. I cannot continue to live with a man I do not love. He will not accept the child I'm carrying, indeed I believe he will reject Amanda too. My love, we reap what we sow, and I fear that this will end badly.'

The remainder of the letter was so blurred she could not read on. She sank on to the window seat, clutching the paper to her chest, ashen faced. 'Oh! You know what this means? Amanda is not his child.' Cassie swallowed the bile that rose in to her throat as something far worse occurred to her. 'This letter was never sent. It has lain hidden in here for the past three years. She says she was going to pack her bags, run away to join whoever this Robert is, so how did she end up with a broken neck from falling off her horse?'

Ann was looking as shocked as she

was. 'I have no idea, but there must be a reasonable explanation, it cannot be what you're thinking, what we're both thinking.'

'I cannot marry him, not now, not until he has explained the whole to me. I shall have to ask him what happened.'

'Cassie, you must not do that, it will be tantamount to accusing your future husband of murder. He would never forgive you, guilty or not. You will have to hold your tongue.'

Cassie did make a decision, and not the one Ann expected. 'I'm going to take this letter with me. Let's leave these rooms, I don't wish anyone else to know we've been in here. He must have locked the door from the inside and told the staff not to enter.'

With shaking fingers she folded the letter and pushed it inside her long sleeve. There was a slight bulge, but she doubted anyone would suspect what she had hidden. They hurried from the bedchamber and closed the door, locking it carefully. Cassie fled back to her own rooms, her heart breaking, but determined to follow the course she had decided on.

'I must return to the schoolroom, my dear, will you be all right on your own?'

'Of course I shall. Amanda must not suspect anything. Whatever happens, we must make sure she doesn't suffer any more than she already has.'

Her brow furrowed and she sank on to the *chaise-longue*. She dropped her head into her hands trying to clear her mind, trying to understand what she had learnt. She knew now that Amanda was not Jonathan's true daughter, which explained why he had been spending so much time away from her, why he appeared to avoid physical contact with the child. It also explained his serious demeanour, and why he rarely laughed and always had a hidden sadness in his eyes.

To have been so cruelly used, it didn't bear thinking about. He had married his wife because he had loved her only to discover she not only loved another, but had produced her lover's child and foisted it off as his. At the time of her death, his wife was carrying a second bastard — and the father was a vicar! It was small wonder that he had turned against God, refused to attend church. How could a man of the cloth have behaved so reprehensibly?

She sat back, knowing what she had to do. When Jonathan returned she would give him the letter and let him explain what had happened. It was possible that he had, in his justifiable rage, killed his wife and then disguised it as a riding accident. She knew she couldn't burn the letter, pretend she'd never read it — even if by so doing everyone could be happy; she could marry the man she loved; he would find happiness and Amanda would have two loving parents again. No, whatever the outcome, Cassie had to be certain Jonathan did not have more blood on his hands than the death of her abductor.

10

Cassie tried to pretend that nothing was wrong. She was determined Amanda should not have her happiness ruined until it was absolutely necessary — the little girl was so overjoyed at the thought of having a new mama. She prayed that Jonathan could give her the answer she needed in order that their union could go ahead as planned.

Two day dresses arrived the morning that Jonathan was expected home. Cassie was in her sitting room when the parcel was brought up to her by a footman. Ann and Amanda were sitting with her, having just returned from their morning constitutional.

Amanda was the only one excited by the smart box and layers of tissue. 'Shall I lift a gown out for you, Mama?' Cassie flinched, but she hadn't the heart to reprimand the child for using that term prematurely.

'Yes, darling, do so. You are more knowledgeable on the subject of new garments than either Miss Roberts or I.'

Inside were two beautiful gowns, plus all that was necessary to make a perfect ensemble. These were the sort of garments Cassie had always dreamed of owning. They might live in the middle of nowhere but Madame was an expert in her craft. In spite of her worry she was stirred as Amanda held up the first dress, made of a heavy woven cotton in palest gold. It had a high neck and was pleated over the bosom, and the whole finished with a dark gold sash. Cassie saw that the same dark gold ribbon edged the points of the long sleeves and was sewn around the hem. 'I shall put this on immediately.'

Molly, hearing the excitement in the parlour had come through to see what all the fuss was about. 'Oh, miss, what a lovely gown.'

Cassie hurried into her bedchamber to change leaving the other two to rummage around in the box and remove the matching slippers, silk stockings (which were embroidered with little gold stars) and a gold cashmere shawl which would complete the outfit to perfection.

Amanda gathered the items up and ran to the bedroom door. She was about to burst in but remembered in time that she was supposed to knock. She waited until she was given leave to enter. 'Here are your slippers, stockings and a lovely wrap in the softest of material.'

Cassie, who was standing in her undergarments, waved towards the bed. 'Please put them on there, Amanda, and wait outside with Miss Roberts, I shall come in a moment to parade before you and receive your applause.'

When she appeared in her new finery she received the acclaim she expected. She twirled, sending the skirts spinning out in a cloud of gold around her feet. 'Mama, you look like a princess. Papa will wonder who you are.'

Ann removed her charge to the schoolroom as soon as they heard the sound of carriage wheels crunching on the gravel at the front of the house. 'I believe it's your father coming home. We shall all meet again for afternoon tea. Come down to the drawing room at four.'

Cassie prayed that this would take place as planned. If things went badly with Jonathan, then God knows where they would all be that afternoon. She couldn't settle, but wandered around picking up and putting down the ornaments, one ear cocked for his arrival.

She had decided to confront him in the privacy of her own rooms. She did not wish the ever-vigilant servants to hear what was said between them.

★ ★ ★

Fifteen minutes after his arrival Jonathan was in his chambers hastily changing from his travel-stained garments. Although he'd travelled in a closed carriage, he'd had to get out and push when they had become stuck in a deep rut, and he was mired to his knees. All the way home his heart had been rejoicing at his good fortune.

He intended to tell his future wife the sad story of his first marriage, but not today, he didn't want to spoil his homecoming. In the few days he'd been away he'd had time to reflect on the seven miserable years he had been married to Lydia. He had married her in good faith, captivated by her dark hair, beautiful green eyes, and lively personality. He had imagined himself neck over crop in love with her, and even when she seemed reluctant to accept his advances, he hadn't taken no for an answer. He had assumed it was maidenly modesty, and when her parents had assured him their daughter was delighted with his attentions he decided to make her an offer. When he had declared himself, she had accepted him prettily, and three months after they were betrothed they had been married.

From the beginning it had been a disaster. He had done his best to initiate her gently into the marriage bed, indeed had waited several days before consummating the union. But she had not enjoyed his lovemaking, turning away in tears each time, until he had ceased to visit, mystified by her attitude and heartbroken that his marriage appeared to be over before it had begun. He started travelling away from home for weeks at a time, finding it too hard to be with the woman he loved and not be able to make love to her.

When his daughter had been born he had been overjoyed and he didn't care that his lovely child looked like neither of them. Amanda more than made up for the lack of affection he got from his wife. Lydia insisted on going to London for the season each year, and although he sometimes accompanied her for a few weeks, he found the constant bowing

167

and scraping, the overheated rooms, the smell of over-perfumed unwashed humanity, too much for his country soul.

He had a fine townhouse and was happy to leave his wife to enjoy herself, for when she returned at the end of the season each year she was always more relaxed, happy, and for a while she would receive him in her bedroom, if not with willingness, then with some degree of enjoyment.

When Amanda was six, things changed. Lydia had come back early from her visit to town, her face pale, and had immediately made it plain that he would be welcome in her bedroom. By this time his love had drained away and he refused her offer. Unless she became his wife in every sense she could remain celibate as he did. Instead of accommodating her wishes he had gone away on business, not returning for several weeks.

His knuckles whitened as he remembered what he had discovered on his return. He had gone to his wife's chambers, deciding to try one last time, for Amanda's sake, at a reconciliation. He had entered unannounced, as was his right, and found her in a negligee, the windows wide open blowing the flimsy material close about her naked body. Even to someone as untutored in such matters as he, he could see at once that she was with child.

He pushed the memories of that horrible day to the back of his mind, to be resurrected at a more suitable time. Now he would visit his beloved Cassie, and shower her with the gifts he'd bought her. He hadn't gone to Norwich on business at all; he'd gone to buy her a betrothal ring and some other jewellery appropriate to her station.

He turned to his valet. 'Samuel, is Miss Forsythe downstairs or in her private apartment?'

'I believe that she's in her rooms, sir.'

Jonathan gathered together his parcels and, his eyes alight with love, his mouth curving in a smile he headed for her chambers.

Cassie turned at the knock and bade

him enter. He came in, and the love on his face almost made her change her mind. He came forward, arms outstretched, expecting her to run into them. Somehow she held herself immobile, and instead of a kiss from her she held out the letter.

'What is this, my dear? Is something wrong? You seem . . . well you don't seem like yourself today.'

She couldn't speak. Unshed tears were clogging her throat as she pushed the paper into his hand and turned her back to stand, facing out across the park. She noticed it was beginning to sleet and the wind was moaning around the eaves.

She heard him opening the letter. There was complete silence and she knew he must be reading. Then she heard him fold the letter and waited for his comment.

'Why have you given me this?' His question was spoken softly, but she detected an edge of steel in his voice.

She spun, her eyes huge. 'Why do

you think? I want you to explain what happened on the day your wife died. I cannot marry you until I know the truth.'

His eyes narrowed and he drew himself to his full, formidable height. When he spoke his eyes were hard, his voice icy. 'I thought better of you, Miss Forsythe. I have no intention of answering or explaining anything to you. You obviously do not trust me. Our liaison is at an end. I expect you to leave my home this afternoon.' He said no more, but turned and strode out leaving her bereft.

Her knees buckled and she collapsed on to the window seat. Whatever she had expected to happen, it had not been this. He had been so cold, as if he hated her. Why hadn't he answered, told her what she wished to know? She sat there stunned for a few moments, unable to assimilate the disaster she had caused. He had told her to leave his house, but where could she go? It was already almost noon and sleeting heavily — she only had two decent garments to her name, and little money to support herself.

She rang the bell and Molly appeared. 'What's wrong, miss, you look as if you seen a ghost.'

'Molly, fetch Miss Roberts to me immediately, Miss Amanda must stay in the schoolroom.'

She paced the room, unable to think coherently. Should she go and beg for his forgiveness, ask him . . . well what could she ask him? By giving him the letter she'd accused him of having a hand in his wife's untimely death. What had possessed her to something so stupid?

All she had to do was ask him, not pass him the letter in that melodramatic fashion. She had only herself to blame for his reaction. Whether he was guilty no longer mattered. She had mishandled the situation and must live with the consequences.

Ann came to her and on hearing what had transpired shook her head.

'My dear, I told you not to confront him. Don't look so worried, I shall come with you. Nanny can take care of Miss Amanda, after all she has been doing so quite successfully these past few months. I shall get Mary to pack my things, you get Molly to pack yours. I'm certain Mr Anderson will allow you to use his carriage. He's not a monster, just a man whose heart you've broken into pieces.'

Cassie sat like a person in a trance; she didn't know what to say to Amanda, so decided to say nothing. Instead she wrote a note telling her how much she loved her, apologizing for having to leave, and hoping that one day she would understand and forgive her.

Two hours after her disastrous interview she was climbing into his carriage, which was still dirty from his recent return from Norwich. She saw tears in the housekeeper's eyes as she left, and Tom, who was driving the coach, seemed incapable of speech. She was unaware of the worsening weather and as the coach trundled away the tears she'd managed to hold back began to flow.

They were scarcely at the end of the drive before she was sobbing uncontrollably against Ann's shoulder. Molly sat opposite, clucking and tutting, but unable to offer her any solace. The weather was so bad Ann ordered Tom to change direction and head for The Black Sheep, not to Ipswich.

'We shall wait outside, Tom, if you could kindly go in and see if they have rooms for us, for tonight or until the weather improves and we can continue our journey?'

The man nodded, his face sombre. 'I'll be happy to do that, Miss Roberts. A right bad show this is. I don't like to speak ill of the master, but what is he thinking, sending you out into the cold like this?'

Somehow Cassie managed to control her misery, dry her eyes and, with the deep brim of her bonnet disguising her distress, she hurried into the inn and upstairs to the rooms they had been allocated. They were adequate, no more than that, but better than being out in the sleet with no roof over her head at all.

She retired immediately to bed, leaving Ann to organise matters and arrange for their meals to be sent up. Her pillow was sodden when eventually she fell asleep, not knowing where she would be the following week, or what she would live on. Sir John was still her guardian, she still had no access to her inheritance and only a few pounds in savings. She knew that Ann had little more. This would keep them going for a few weeks, but after that they would be destitute unless one or both of them found suitable employment.

* * *

Jonathan repaired to his study and grabbed the brandy decanter, filling his crystal glass to the brim. He downed it in one gulp, filling it a second time. Only after several glasses did his hurt become bearable. Even in death, Lydia had reached out to ruin his life. Why hadn't he had her room cleared out? It wasn't as if he'd left it as a memorial to her, merely that he'd chosen to ignore her very existence in the hope that his fury would abate.

At first he had been determined to discover who Robert was and kill him. But his daughter was inconsolable at her mother's death, and by the time she had recovered, so had he. The man, whoever he was, must know of Lydia's death and be suffering torments of his own. But now . . . how could this have happened? Just when he thought he had happiness in his grasp it was snatched away again so cruelly. He reached out for the decanter and finding it empty hurled it in a drunken fury into the fire. The resulting explosion of glass and alcohol brought the butler running to the study.

Foster burst in, not stopping to

knock. 'Can I be of assistance, sir?'

Jonathan stared at the shards of glass sticking into his boots and scattered over the fireplace and nodded. 'I need another decanter of brandy, now. And send someone in to clear up this mess.'

He continued to drink until oblivion claimed him. He slept, slumped in his chair, and didn't wake up until his valet came in late the following morning. He sat up. His head hurt like the very devil. How much had he drunk, for God's sake? Then he felt several sharp stabs on his legs and looked down in astonishment at the glass embedded in his Hessians.

What the hell had been going on here? He had no recollection of throwing the decanter, no recollection of anything apart from drinking more brandy than was good him. Samuel approached him warily, his usual smile absent.

'Shall I remove those boots for you, sir, before you do yourself any more hurt?' His valet's voice was distant. What had he done to offend him?

He stretched out his legs and watched as his man knelt and carefully removed the splinters before pulling off his boots. He looked down with interest at his blood-soaked stockings.

'Shall I send for the doctor to attend to those cuts, sir?'

'Damn the physician, you can attend to me. I need to go back to my rooms. Run me a bath, and bring me a pot of black coffee and something to eat.'

He walked in his red-stained stockings through the house and, even with a crashing headache, detected looks of disapproval and a decidedly chilly atmosphere from all the staff he met. Mystified by their behaviour, he reached his chambers and flopped down in front of the fire. He heard the clanking and banging of buckets being brought to fill his bath but no sign of food or the coffee. Impatiently he stood up, wincing from the pain in his legs. What had possessed him to drink so much? Why did he have a sinking feeling in his stomach?

His stomach lurched again and he knew he was about to cast up his accounts. Forgetting all else he shot into his bedchamber, reaching the china basin just in time. He dropped the rest of his garments on the floor, seeing at once that the cuts on his legs were superficial and needed no more attention than a wash.

Submerging himself in the lemon scented water he closed his eyes, trying to remember what had happened the previous day. His legs stung unpleasantly but he ignored it. A few minutes later a steaming mug of well-sweetened coffee was handed to him in silence. As he sipped the drink his digestion settled and his head slowly cleared.

Suddenly he erupted from the bath sending a cascade of water over the floor. 'My God! I sent her away. What was I thinking of? Tell me, Sam, tell me that I didn't do anything so stupid. Tell me I didn't behave with as little compassion as her uncle.'

His valet looked at him and shook his

head. 'I'm sorry, sir, but I cannot do that. Yesterday you told Miss Forsythe to leave the house and she did so, taking Molly and Miss Roberts with her.'

'Quickly man, get me something to wear. I must find her, the weather is worsening . . . she has no money . . . I am a brute of the very worst kind.' Sam didn't disagree.

Twenty minutes later he was dressed and waiting for his stallion to be brought round to him. He had already spoken to Tom and knew that his beloved was at The Black Sheep. He thanked God that the ladies had had the sense stay there. He realised that if it hadn't been sleeting so heavily, if the road had been dry, then she might well have continued on to Ipswich, caught the mail coach and be lost to him.

In spite of his anguish, his remorse, he knew that he had not been abandoned by his maker as he'd feared. He had been taught a lesson, reminded that losing his temper was not the way a sensible man carried on. As he was about to leave he turned to Foster. 'Have Tom follow me with the carriage. I shall be returning with Miss Forsythe, Miss Roberts and her maid within the hour. Have their rooms prepared.' It was only then that he though of Amanda. 'Does Miss Amanda know that Miss Forsythe has left?'

'No, sir, Miss Forsythe left a note, but we ... that is ... well, sir, we decided it would be best not to give it to her, to leave it for a day or so and see how things turned out.' To the butler's astonishment Jonathan stepped forward and gripped him by the shoulders. 'Thank you, Foster, I am forever in your debt. You did the right thing. I wish to God that I had done so.'

* * *

Cassie woke the next morning to hear the gentle rhythm of another's breathing at her side and turned her head lethargically. Ann was still asleep, but she could no longer lie in bed — she needed to get up, she needed to think about their future, about both their futures.

She walked over to the window and peered around the curtain. It was just light, and looked to be fine and dry. The courtyard below the window was already busy with folk coming and going. It was a pity the mail coach didn't call, then they wouldn't have to make their way to Ipswich somehow, and catch it from there. But where would they go? She had no idea. Yes — she did! Sir John and Lady Digby had fled to the continent in fear of their lives, leaving Upton Manor to Peregrine. They could go there. He would be pleased to see them, and she could take care of him, make sure he had what he wanted, wasn't bothered by trivia and wasn't taken advantage of by tradesmen or staff.

She turned to the sleeping figure on the bed. 'Ann, wake up, we have to get ready to leave. We're going back to Upton Manor. Now that my uncle and aunt are gone, I can live there comfortably and take charge of the house for my cousin.'

Ann sat up rubbing her eyes. 'I had already thought of that, and was going to suggest it this morning. In fact, we haven't unpacked the trunks. They are waiting downstairs for the carter. There's a mail coach leaves from Ipswich at 11 o'clock, hopefully we can obtain seats on it..'

'I think it must be a little after seven now. We can be ready within the hour.' She smiled grimly, from now on she would be beholden to no one. She had thrown away her one chance of happiness and didn't deserve another.

★   ★   ★

At eleven o'clock Jonathan thundered into the yard of the inn, leapt from the saddle and ran in to greet the flustered landlord. 'Miss Forsythe, Miss Roberts — are they here?'

'I'm sorry, Mr Anderson, sir, but they

left early this morning. They're catching a mail coach from Ipswich.' He looked at the tall clock ticking noisily against the wall. 'In fact, sir, they will already be on their way.'

11

The mail coach left, as it always did, precisely on the hour. Cassie was huddled in the corner seat, pressing her face against the side of the carriage and trying not to think about the last time she'd travelled in such a vehicle. Ann was sitting by her side, and Molly next to her. The coach was jammed, both inside and out, with the usual travellers — farmers, clerics, but this time no military gentleman. They bounced over the cobbled streets of Ipswich heading for the toll road and Cassie thought wryly that the two young officers would not have ignored her now, not dressed as she was and with two females in attendance.

She raised her damp eyes to meet the sympathetic stare of a middle-aged woman sitting, with her husband, directly opposite. Instantly she looked down again, burying her trembling fingers in her muff. She supposed that she looked what she was, a young woman fleeing from someone or something she could no longer cope with. Why else would a lady dressed so expensively travel by the common mail coach?

They stopped briefly to change horses but the passengers did not alight. Their first break for refreshments, and to use whatever primitive facilities were available, was at Colchester at The Red Lion in the High Street. Last time they had stayed there for twenty-five minutes, time enough to grab something to eat and scramble back in before the coach left. She closed her eyes, resting her head on the squabs, trying to make sense of what had happened but failing miserably. When the coach arrived in Colchester, the steps were let down and she was first to escape the stuffy interior. Keeping her head lowered, her ravaged face hidden inside her bonnet brim, she continued to step forward but unexpectedly cannoned into a solid wall of flesh.

She drew a deep steadying breath, instantly recognizing with whom she had collided. Her eyes flew up to meet Jonathan's. How had he come here? She didn't know if she should turn and flee, and swayed in indecision, as if about to swoon.

★ ★ ★

'God dammit to hell! This is all my fault.'

Without another word he bent and swept her up into his arms holding her tight to his chest, much to her consternation, Molly and Ann's delight and the amusement of the rest of passengers. Ignoring the spectators, he strode into the inn to the private parlour he had already reserved. His mad ride to beat the coach had almost killed his horse, but it was worth it.

Placing her tenderly on a chair he

swung round and slammed the door in the faces of her companions. Then he turned back, dropping to his knees in front of her.

'How can you ever forgive me? What I did to you yesterday was unforgivable.'

She looked up, her face pinched, her eyes brimming with tears and he felt the weight of guilt crush him. He'd done some terrible things in his time. He knew he could have handled things better when his wife had revealed her infidelity; that he shouldn't have killed Cassie's abductor in cold blood. Turning the woman he loved more than his very life out into the winter to fend for herself was by far the worst.

She sat limp in her chair, head lowered, her hands hidden inside a silly muff. For a moment he was unsure what to do, then slowly she raised her head and spoke to him.

'I'm so sorry. I should never have doubted you, you're an honourable man — I know you would never harm a woman, whatever she'd done to betray you. I don't understand what you're doing here, but I thank God that you are, and that I have been given the chance to offer my apologies for doubting you.'

For a moment he was speechless. Then, his heart bursting with joy, he snatched her from the chair and leaning his back against the wall, pulled her almost roughly onto his lap. With trembling fingers he undid the bow that held her ghastly bonnet in place and tossed it over his shoulder. The muff followed.

'My darling Cassie — sweetheart — it's I who must beg your forgiveness. I don't know what I was thinking of yesterday to send you away like that. I should have told you what had happened the day that Lydia died — what else could you think, having read her letter, than that I had some hand in her death?'

He felt her relax and one small hand crept up to touch his face. 'I don't care what you did, it's in the past. I realised last night that when you love someone, you love them completely, and that is how I love you. You don't have to tell me what happened if you don't want to.'

'I want to tell you — it's quite simple really.' He settled her more comfortably on his lap and began his sorry tale. 'Lydia wrote that letter just after I'd stormed out. I shouted, vented my spleen, but I didn't raise my hand to her. I might have looked murderous, but I would never have harmed her.' He paused and she remained quiet waiting for him to continue.

'When she had finished writing the letter she must have decided to mail it herself. What you found was a draft — obviously she decided she couldn't send it as it was, so she rewrote it. Foster told me she came downstairs, apparently calm, and asked for her mare to be brought round. She galloped off down the drive and no one saw her alive again. When I got back it was to find pandemonium at the house.'

'What happened?'

'Peter Hodgkin, my estate manager, had discovered her horse and was organising the male servants to search for her. As I was already mounted I rode ahead and was able to see over the hedges. I saw her body lying on the far side of a five barred gate. She had obviously fallen and broken her neck.'

He felt her shifting her weight and then she tugged on his lapels, pulling his head down towards her waiting lips. As he kissed her he felt the guilt trickle away and knew he had been given another chance. For some reason she was prepared to forgive him, still loved him in spite of his brutality. He drew back to smile down at her and her face was transformed. From ashen to radiant in the space of a few minutes.

'Jonathan, you're a good man, but you could be a better father. You must promise me that from this point on you'll forget how Amanda arrived in this world and treat her as your own

191

daughter. Treat her as you will any children that we may be blessed with.'

That was an easy promise to make. 'I do love her, and since you came into our lives it has become easier for both of us. You are a Godsend, and although I said we should marry at Martlesham Hall I should like to say our vows in the local church with friends and family present.'

She didn't need to answer him; her smile told him everything he needed to know.

THE END

We do hope that you have enjoyed reading this large print book.

Did you know that all of our titles are available for purchase?

We publish a wide range of high quality large print books including:
Romances, Mysteries, Classics
General Fiction
Non Fiction and Westerns

Special interest titles available in large print are:
The Little Oxford Dictionary
Music Book, Song Book
Hymn Book, Service Book

Also available from us courtesy of Oxford University Press:
Young Readers' Dictionary
(large print edition)
Young Readers' Thesaurus
(large print edition)

For further information or a free brochure, please contact us at:
Ulverscroft Large Print Books Ltd.,
The Green, Bradgate Road, Anstey,
Leicester, LE7 7FU, England.
Tel: (00 44) **0116 236 4325**
Fax: (00 44) **0116 234 0205**

Other titles in the
Linford Romance Library:

PALE ORCHID

Mavis Thomas

Bethany delays her hopes of rescuing a failing relationship while she helps a friend by working at The Corner Cattery. But there are unexpected problems. She becomes involved with twin brothers and the bitter feud between them: Dominic the successful but troubled and moody playwright; Darryl the dedicated doctor torn between his work in Africa and his two motherless children. Many conflicts must be resolved, and searching questions answered, before Bethany can see clearly her road ahead.